BREATHE

V.W. SMITH

Copyright © 2024 by V.W. Smith
Breathe A Club F.O.U.R.S. Novel
First publication: June 2024
Cover Photography: Ashley Cardenas of Meraki Rose Photography
Cover Design: Caitlin Cain and V.W. Smith
Formatting: V.W. Smith and Lori Smith
Editing: V.W. Smith and Lori Smith

All rights reserved. No part of this book may be reproduced in any form or by any electronic or mechanical means, including information storage and retrieval systems, without written permission from the author, except for the use of brief quotations in a book review. The unauthorized reproduction or distribution of copyrighted work is illegal. Criminal copyright infringement, including infringement without monetary gain, is investigated by the FBI and is punishable by fines and federal imprisonment. Please purchase only authorized electronic editions and do not participate in, or encourage, the electronic piracy of copyrighted materials. Your support of the author's rights is appreciated. This book is a work of fiction. Names, characters, places, brands, and incidents are the products of the author's imagination or used fictitiously. Any resemblance to actual events, locales, or persons, living or dead, is entirely coincidental.

CONTENTS

1. Trigger Warning — 1
2. Note From Author — 3
3. Prologue — 5
4. Chapter 1 — 10
5. Chapter 2 — 18
6. Chapter 3 — 25
7. Chapter 4 — 33
8. Chapter 5 — 39
9. Chapter 6 — 41
10. Chapter 7 — 49
11. Chapter 8 — 54
12. Chapter 9 — 60
13. Chapter 10 — 66
14. Chapter 11 — 70
15. Chapter 12 — 76
16. Chapter 13 — 80
17. Chapter 14 — 95
18. Chapter 15 — 108
19. Chapter 16 — 114
20. Chapter 17 — 120
21. Chapter 18 — 127
22. Chapter 19 — 134
23. Chapter 20 — 144
24. Chapter 21 — 153
25. Chapter 22 — 162
26. Chapter 23 — 170
27. Chapter 24 — 177
28. Chapter 25 — 188
29. Chapter 26 — 199

30.	Chapter 27	207
31.	Chapter 28	220
32.	Chapter 29	231
33.	Chapter 30	246
34.	Epilogue	254
	Acknowledgments	259
	About The Author	261

TRIGGER WARNING

Trigger Warnings (Some may call it their shopping list):

Sexually explicit scenes (Including: BDSM, Sex Clubs, MF, MM, MMF)
Sexual Assault mentioned (Not to main characters)
Anxiety & anxiety attacks
Therapy Deep dives
Degradation
Prior Intimate partner abuse & violence
Assault
Emotional abuse
Profanity
Fatphobia
Misogyny
Physical abuse
Child abuse

V.W. SMITH

(This will be in a flashback and involves emotional abuse and Abandonment)
Depression
Self-harm

NOTE FROM AUTHOR

Note from the Author:

Thank you so much for choosing to go on this journey with me. This book is dear to my heart as it is my first. Please keep your own sanity and mental health in mind when reading this book, as we will be diving into both trauma and healing. Doing this will include therapy scenes, processing, and struggling through it. Don't give up on it. Promise it's worth it!

Sidenote:
If you are family, I'm not going to tell you to turn back now.
I am, however, going to tell you...
This is personality number two...

V.W. SMITH

Don't tell her you read this...
It'll make things awkward for all of us!

PROLOGUE

3 MONTHS AGO

*T*HE ATMOSPHERE IN THE CLUB TONIGHT IS HEADY.

I can taste the salt from sweat in the air, and feel the buzz of sex on my skin.

"Color, Sweetheart?" Harrison asks.

"Green, Sir. Thank you, Sir," I pant out in a quiet voice.

"Good girl, but remember my sweet girl, speak up so I can hear you fully," he coos.

I roll my eyes and say in a loud voice "Green, Sir. Thank you, Sir!" The smack across my ass comes faster than I was ready for.

"Acting like a brat will get you nothing but a sore ass and an aching pussy that will find no relief tonight," Harrison growls. "Remember, obedient girls get rewarded, naughty girls get to squirm." Shit, why does that do so much for me?

I feel the wind shift just before the leather of the flogger snaps against my back.

"Six," I moan. There is something so freeing feeling the sting of the flogger and letting myself just feel. The sting shoots down my back again and I feel that floating space setting in.

"Seven," and again, "eight," at this point I no longer feel the sting. Each kiss of the leather feels like another gust of air in my lungs.

"Nine," I gasp out not knowing if Harrison can even hear me anymore.

"Last one, Sweetheart," I hear Harrison say in the breathy tone he gets when he's turned on, "and yes, you may cum." The air shifts again, but this time the tails hit right between my legs. Darkness engulfs me and stars explode behind my eyes and I feel like I am lost amongst the galaxy. If I didn't have so much trust in Harrison I would be terrified, but knowing he always has my back, I let my climax swell through me with vigor.

When I finally start coming to, I can hear Harrison chuckling darkly. Uh oh, he only gets that tone when he's feeling especially dirty. "Ten, Sir. Thank you, Sir," I finally gasp out. "Oh, you're very welcome, Sweetheart, can you give me a color?" he says.

"Green still, Sir, very, very green," I say with as much power as I have. I'm breathing hard so I know it must be difficult to understand me. "That's my perfect girl. Now focus on your breathing while I remove your restraints. I don't want you passing out before I get at least 3 more out of you."

I feel more than see him releasing the cuffs around my

wrists and ankles. I'm beyond grateful that he chose the padded cuffs tonight. I have meetings tomorrow and it is way too warm to have to wear long sleeves. Harrison helps me roll on to my back on the large bed in the voyeur room and starts slowly rubbing my ankles to help me relax. As I look around us, I see that the small audience we started with has almost doubled in size. My heart rate begins to pick up speed again as I feel the panic creeping in. As much as I love knowing people are watching, knowing and actually seeing are two very different things.

I feel Harrison moving up my body but I can't seem to pull my focus from the crowd around us. Grabbing my chin he moves my face so he is the only thing in my field of view. "Focus on me, Sweetheart, only on me." I feel his other hand sliding up my side to my breast. He uses his fingertip to trace a circle around my nipple. "Count with me Rose, how many circles will it take?"

Chills spread across my skin as I began to sink into his gaze, the feeling of his finger circling with almost no pressure bringing me back to the present. "1..2..3..4..5.. Uhhhh, Sir, please." I'm putty in his hands. "Please what, Sweetheart? What do you need?" He says with a deep growl. All I can do is groan. Doesn't he know he makes it impossible to focus?

I hear the slap before the sting ever registers on my breast. "YOU," I gasp, "You, Sir, I need you!" My body feels like a pile of coals ready to ignite, one more spark in the right direction and I'll burst into flames. "I can feel you ready to burst, Sweetheart, so this next one will be fast and hard. Do you understand?" I nod like a crazy person. I don't care how we get there, I just need to be there. Now! "Words, Rose, or I will drag this out". I answer in an irritated growl "Yes, Sir, I understand! Now, please!"

He enters me in one forceful thrust, chuckling under his breath. "I'm giving you what you need now, but don't think you won't pay for that attitude, brat." I have no doubt I will pay for it and look forward to it. It only takes two more deep strokes before I can feel my climax clawing its way through my body, starting at my toes.

Is the bed vibrating? Wait, no, I think that's me. Damn, this is going to be huge. "Sir, please. I need, please, I need..." Hey, I never said I was above begging. "Not yet, Rose, hold on for me." Is he crazy, how does he expect me to hold this off? "Sir, I can't, please, please let me cum!" My desperation is evident in my voice.

"Let go, baby. Now!" Just like that my body bursts into flames. I swear I can taste the sweet tang of smoke. I feel him pull out and, in the back of my mind I register the guttural sound of Harrison reaching his own climax. The feeling of his seed striking my heated core adds fuel to the inferno that is my body.

Harrison collapses on the bed and rolls me into him. Stroking my back, he starts the process of bringing me down. He's whispering quietly in my ear, but I'm not registering what he's saying. He is always so sweet; I wish we could be more than just friends, but apparently that must not be in the stars for us, no matter how I feel for him.

Finally, feeling like I'm back in the real world, I look up into his eyes, "Thank you, Harrison, that was amazing." Showing me his thousand watt smile, he responds, "No

Sweetheart, I can guarantee you the pleasure was all mine," with that cocky wink of his.

Just then, all of the above lights come on, blasting the room with harsh lighting, ruining the sensual atmosphere. "What the fuck?" I panic, grabbing the sheet to cover my body. No matter what Harrison or anyone else says, no one wants to see this body in this harsh lighting. "Language," Harrison snaps. All I can do is roll my eyes. "Watch it sweets," Harrison snips in his Dom voice as he glares at me. "Stay here and drink some of your water, I'm going to see what's going on."

"Yes, Sir," I say. Harrison opens the door and an ear piercing scream tears through the room. I'm on my feet and running after Harrison before I can even register what's happening. I would know the voice of my best friend anywhere.... I need to get to Kat and I need to get to her now.

CHAPTER 1

ROSE

Noooooo.... the irritating sound of my alarm going off pulls me out of my dreams. Dammit, I was about to be put in one heck of a quadruple decker man sandwich. I roll over and feel something cold touch my arm. Well no, wonder I was dreaming of being the banana in that split. I fell asleep reading *The Saviors* again. My girl Ames Mills knows how to give you all the spicy feels.

Shuffling over to my alarm across the room, I slam the off button. I hate mornings, if I didn't put the stupid thing over here I'm not sure I would ever get up on time. I sure wouldn't be up at 5:30 in the morning.

I grab my phone and head to the bathroom to start my morning routine. Hitting the play button on my music app, I relieve myself then reach over and turn my shower on to lava. Since I have to wait for the shower to heat up, I go to the kitchen and pour myself a huge cup of coffee, extra strength (duh). I may not be able to afford much but this is one thing that I will always keep in stock in this kitchen. Two spoons of sugar, and an obscene amount of my favorite vanilla caramel creamer later, and I have the nectar of the gods. Taking greedy sips, I head back into the bathroom to shower.

Setting the mug down on the shelf, I quickly strip and jump in. Yeah that's right, if people can have a shower beer, I'm having shower coffee. Standing under the scalding water, I drink my coffee and run through everything I have to do today. I know I have meetings starting at 9 am, then I'm leaving early for therapy at 2 pm. *Sigh,* I need to get a hustle on if I want to have any time to prepare for my meetings.

After quickly washing my body, I use the water in my hands to loosen up the tangles in my hair. I finish drying off quickly, wrapping my towel around myself as I take the 3 steps to the small sink. I don't recognize the woman staring back at me in the mirror. *Who is she?* I see the darkness and sadness looming behind her eyes. No, I don't have time to focus on that right now. I grab my brush, and throw my hair into a quick ponytail, before blowing through a basic makeup look.

Walking back to the room we share, I look over to Kat's bed. Nine weeks that bed has been empty, I miss my best friend. I've seen her a few times since she went to the treatment center, and I'm both excited and terrified for her to get to come home next week. I've felt lost without her here. Don't get me wrong I'm glad she's getting the help she needs, but selfishly, I miss my other half.

For the last fifteen years, she has been the one I went to with everything. I needed to talk something out? Call Kat.

Bored and just want to chat? Call Kat. See something funny? Call Kat. Running errands or want to go on a random adventure? Kidnap Kat. Heck, she's the person I would call just to sit on the phone and body double with me, just so I didn't feel alone in getting things done.

When she finally moved to Austin from Missouri, where we grew up, after I had lived here by myself for almost two years, I was ecstatic. She needed to escape her asshole ex and I was all too happy to have my person with me again. Now, I wonder if it had all been a huge mistake. She's only been here for 8 months and now she's in the hospital.

Pulling myself out of my head, I walk over to the dresser and take my ADHD and anxiety meds, then head into the closet to dress. I put on my favorite high waisted trouser jeans and a pretty royal blue blouse. Staring at my shoes, I try to think about just how much I'm going to have to walk around today. Deciding it was not much, I grab my 'I'm a baddie and can handle anything' pencil heel booties'. I love these things. They are like if biker boots and stilettos had a child, but they are what my Granny used to call 4 hour shoes. Walk around too long and your toes will be screaming.

Looking over, I see the clock reads 6:52 am. Crap, I've gotta get going. I grab my mug out of the bathroom on my way to the kitchen, place it in the sink, and fill my travel mug to the brim. Double checking that my laptop, Kindle, and headphones are all in my bag, I head to the door, grabbing my keys and wallet on the way out.

Traffic was horrible this morning. My usual thirty minute commute took an hour, which leaves me with only one hour to prepare for my regular morning check-in meeting and my fleet meeting. Walking into our office I smile at my lead.

"Morning Matt, you're here early!!" I say in my chipper work voice.

"Hey Rose, yeah I came in a little early to get the day set up and catch up on everything since I was out yesterday. I've already updated all the spreadsheets and presentations for the day." I could hear in his voice that something was amiss.

"Cool, well I got all the vehicles with pick up appointments for the day ready last night, along with two extra just in case, since the team up front can't seem to stick to the no walk-ins rule. Oh and I stole Liliana yesterday since it was slow and we did all the dealership runs, and I sent all of the appointment confirmations out, too. Looks like between the two of us we are ahead of the game!" Smiling, I walk over to my desk and start to unload. Matt clears his throat and I know I'm about to get a talking to.

"Yeah, I saw that was all done. Rose, what did I tell you?" He sounded all grumbly so I decided to play with him a bit.

"Ummm, that I'm awesome and a great employee, the absolute best really, and that this place would completely crash without me... OH and that you have no idea what you would do without me?" Throwing him a saccharine smile. I turn to finish setting up my desk for the day.

In his grumbly 'I haven't had enough coffee for your BS' voice he responds "Rose, while that may all be very true, I also told you to stop working late and overworking yourself."

I stop what I'm doing and turn back to him. Giving him a dramatic eye roll, I huff "I didn't overwork myself. I simply made today easier for us."

"First off, don't roll your eyes at me. You know I'm right. Second, you're only required to get morning appointment cars ready the day before, not all of them. Twenty eight cars is way too many to do at one time and by yourself. Third, those dealership runs didn't even need to be done until Friday, and lastly, you sent all of those messages at 8pm, when you are supposed to get off by 5:30!" Oh man, he really is pissed.

"I understand you want to do a great job, but Rose, you're going to burn yourself out and then I'll be stuck here without you. So please, if not for yourself, then for me. Please stop overdoing it. Also, don't think I missed that you clocked out at 6 pm. I checked the camera and you didn't even leave here till after 8:15 pm last night. You will be fixing your timesheet."

Why did he have to use that tone? I don't even think he realizes he's doing it, but when he is irritated with me and it's just us in the office he ends up using the same tone a dom would use in a scene. I swear he knows it's the easiest way to get me to do what he wants.

"BUTTTTTT MATTTTTTT!" I whine "I'm leaving early today AND Thursday. I just want things to go as smoothly as possible!"

Sighing, he gives me his 'I know, but you're still in trouble' look. "I know and I also understand that you are going to be dealing with really heavy crap this week. Hell, I even expected it, but that doesn't make it okay. You get stressed about one thing and throw yourself into work. It's not healthy, hun." With a deep sigh I watch the fight leave his eyes. "Okay fine, I'm done getting on you. This time! Now, go check the microwave, knowing you didn't eat this morning. I brought you a treat."

With a giddy clap I rush from the room straight into our little break area and straight over to the microwave. Popping it open I see two bags from my favorite doughnut place and squeal. Opening the bags I see one has two sausage kolaches and the other has four golden doughnuts. My favorites! Running back into the office I throw my arms around him from behind. All he does is chuckle and wave me off.

Most of the people we work with have said they thought we were secretly dating for years. It wasn't until Kat saw us together and told me that if she didn't know that we saw each other more like siblings than anything else, that she would think we were dating too, that I even realized the way we interacted with each other was strange.

Whatever, at least I didn't have a boss I hated. Plus, he was one of my best friends, I personally would find it weirder if we weren't close. Sitting down, I start eating while I start to check my emails. I need to see if any of our adjusters responded and if any repo appointments needed to be set up.

I'm only a couple minutes into my task when I hear Matt start grumbling to himself. Not even a minute later "Damnit, Rose Marie Morrow! You handled all of the team emails yesterday, too!" Crap! I knew I forgot to mention something.

"Okay, but like you don't have to full name me like that..."

The rest of the morning goes smoothly. We are the number one fleet rental facility in our region again this month and second in the country. It is hard working for a facility that deals with both contracted drivers and a fleet of rental vehicles, but at least I have fun doing it. Most of the time.

Most of my coworkers are wonderful and have even become friends. We hang out after work often and even have an 'off the books' group text. It's great and they always bring the giggles. Everyone except Kate, that is. Kate is the lead up front and she's a royal pain. She stays up everyone's butts all the time but then hides in her office instead of actually helping. Usually, if the team up front needs help, they will find me or Matt. Ugh, I really wish they would drop her like the nasty bag of manure she is.

Around 1pm, I go out to check in with the rest of the team and let them know that I'm about to head out for the day. It's just my luck that as I'm saying it Kate walks out.

"Hmm and where do you think you're going? I don't remember seeing or approving an early out for you on the schedule." I hate her snippy voice and attitude.

Rolling my eyes, I turn to her "Well, as you aren't my lead, you wouldn't see or approve any of my times so that's not really shocking now is it?" Turning away I verify that no one else needs anything from me and start walking back to my office to pack up. I realize Kate is following me and pause. "What can I do for you, Kate?" I say in my most practiced calm tone.

"Oh, I just figured I would make sure your lead actually knows that you're abandoning your job for the day." I chuckle, "Go right ahead, Matt's in the office." She walks ahead of me and I fight back all the hateful words and thoughts running through my head. I'm already wound up about having to go to today's therapy session, I don't need her crap too. I stop walking and take a few deep breaths while I count to 10 in my head. I've got this, I will not choke her out when I walk into my office. I will not let the spawn of Satan's left testicle drive me to the brink today!

Walking into the office, I overhear Matt telling Kate that he is perfectly aware of my comings and goings and that she should focus on her team instead of me. With that I smile and pack up my stuff. Time to head to the day of therapy reckoning.

CHAPTER 2

ROSE

The clock on Dr. Jas' wall ticks loudly, building my irritation further. I know that she's supposed to be one of the best trauma therapists in Central Texas, and I know she's in the lifestyle, but if she doesn't do something about that thing I'm going to have to stop seeing her. "You look agitated Rose, are you not ready to dive into this subject today?" She asks.

"It's not that Jas, usually I can ignore your stupid clock but today I just want to punch it." I know I sound like a complete bitch but she's just gotta deal today.

"Rose, if you don't tell me when things are bothering you, I can't help." She slowly rises off the high back chair she's sitting in and walks over to the wall with the clock. I can't help from following her with my eyes, she is a truly beautiful woman and the way the pencil skirt she's wearing today hugs her ass has my mind running a mile a minute. I quickly shake my head to get my focus back, I seriously need to get laid. I watch as she takes the clock down and removes the battery.

Without looking back at me she says, "You see Rose, simple problems can usually be solved with communication. By you telling me what the problem was, and with just a small amount of work on my part to enact a solution, we have remedied the cause of your irritation." She walks over and sets the clock on her desk before walking back to her chair. "This isn't just something that's useful in my office. Think about when you are with a Dominant and you are negotiating a scene or even during a scene. You have to communicate how you feel about aspects of the scene and how you are handling what is actively going on. Without that communication, trust and boundaries can be broken."

I feel my heart rate speed up and my anger grows hot. "What's the point Jas, when people, even well known Doms, don't listen?!? When you have negotiated and you think that everything is set?!?! When you try to communicate and the person or people who are supposed to listen don't!?!?" I'm practically yelling at this point. My breathing heavy, I can feel the emotions of what I'm saying starting to pull me into a frantic state.

Jas grabs my hand to ground me, "Breathe for me, Rose. Deep breath in through your nose, and slowly out through your mouth. Good, one more, good". I feel myself relax slightly, I knew today was going to be hard and I'm pretty sure I just fell into this woman's trap, damnit.

"Okay, now that you're back with me, are you ready to talk about your feelings from that night?" Her tone is soothing and I know that if things escalate she can bring me down again. "Am I ready, no, but I honestly don't know that I ever will be. I do know I need to though. Kat will be back next week."

"Okay, so walk me through what happened that night. I already know that it has caused you not to trust anymore, but let's dive into the why," I shudder knowing this is going to be rough. "Close your eyes and take me to that night". With a deep breath I shut my eyes and take myself back.

"Kat, Harrison and I decided to go to Peaks that night. Harrison and I wanted to scene and Kat had been vetting a new Dominant, Larry, for a while and they wanted to meet there for their first scene. Usually we would go to F.O.U.R.S, but Larry was only a member at Peaks and said he couldn't afford both. He also got two free guest passes for the night so we only had to pay guest entry for one of us. We thought no big deal, we could explore for one night.

"When we got in all of us grabbed a drink together at the bar, then Kat and Larry grabbed a booth adjacent to us in the lounge and we all sat down to negotiate. When Harrison and I were done with our drinks we stopped by their booth to check in and let them know we would be in the voyeur room. Kat looked so relaxed and excited I didnt think twice about leaving them together. Everything seemed normal.

"Me and Harrison had just finished the first half of our scene and were taking a cool down break when everything seemed to go to shit." My chest begins to tighten again and I feel Jas grab my hand. I open my eyes and feel the tears track down my cheek. "Take a deep breath and then continue, you can do this Rose."

Closing my eyes again I continue. "The main lights came on and we were really confused. As soon as Harrison opened the door to see what was going on, I heard Kat screaming. I didn't have time to think, I knew it was her and I just ran." I take another shuddering breath remembering the scene that I had found.

"When we got to the main room Kat was lying on the floor screaming 'I SAID RED, I SAID RED, I SAID RED' one of the monitors held Larry back with his arms behind his back while two others were trying to get close to her. She wouldn't let them near her, I threw myself around her and she started to fight. I just kept repeating that it was me and I was there. I guess Harrison told the monitors who we were because they didn't try to rip me off of her. When she finally recognized who I was she broke down. 'I said Red, Rose, I told him to stop and he wouldn't.' All I could do was hold her while she shook. I don't know how long we were there but Harrison eventually brought us both our clothes because the police were on their way. I've never seen my best friend that damaged by anything before that night.

"After we dealt with the cops, Harrison took us home. We laid in her bed and she just sobbed. She walked me through everything that happened in their scene, and why she decided to safeword. She said he used tools that she had already told him she wasn't comfortable with. She tried to stop, so they could address it in case he misunderstood her, but he wouldn't let up. She said his exact words were 'You are mine now and I decide when we stop'. She said she screamed red five times before a monitor finally stepped in.

"After she told me that we just laid there together until she finally fell asleep. She didn't get back out of bed for 3 weeks, Jas. She wasn't eating well, not showering, nothing. I finally broke and called her aunt and gave her the high level version of events. Krystal came and Kat was pissed. I knew Krys would be able to do something and she did. Krys got her into an impatient program to work through everything. Kat told me that I had betrayed her and she would never forgive me, and it broke me, but I knew that this would be what was best for her. They left the next morning."

Opening my eyes I stared at Jas, I could feel the dampness on my cheeks but I couldn't bring myself to care. I see the shimmer in Jas`s eyes too. I take a deep breath before she asks, "You know she doesn't actually hate you right?" Well, no shit, I knew that. Me and Kat had already talked that through and we were good with each other now. "Yeah, I know, but I don't think I will ever get the look of just complete brokenness that was on her face out of my head."

Jas nodded "Her attack seems to be hitting you really hard, Rose. What do you think is behind it?"

"I wasn't sure at the time. All I knew is I felt unsafe, at least mentally."

"And now?"

"I've been having nightmares again. I thought we had worked past all of my childhood bullshit but, guess not. I keep dreaming of my mother beating me anytime I did even the smallest thing wrong. Standing over me saying 'I brought you to this world, and I can take you out.' and when I would ask her to stop she would just laugh and tell me 'I'm your mother, I can treat you how I want.'. Other nights I see my father, him with his 'new family'. When I try to explain to him that I want to spend time with just him, because when they are around he doesn't pay any attention to me, he calls me over dramatic and tells me I need to get over it."

"So, based on what you're telling me, Kat's attack, both circumstance and action, has re-traumatized you via Secondary traumatic stress."

Not understanding how I ask "How?"

"Well let's analyze this together," She pauses, looking like she wants to get her wording correct. "You have found solace within the club setting. Dominants, even if they are just your partner for the night, are the authority in a scene. You, as the Submissive, are allowing someone else to take control. You both negotiate and set the boundaries and parameters of what you are comfortable with beforehand. However, even though the Dominant may take the lead in a scene, ultimately the Submissive is the one in control."

"Right" I know how it works.

"The club itself is a controlled environment with a clear set of rules and expectations for everyone, and people there who's entire job is to hold everyone accountable. Giving people a safe space to be free."

"Yes." Where is she going with this?

"By Larry ignoring not only Kat's boundaries but her safeword, he took away the trust a Sub should be able to have with their Dom. No matter how temporary. By him telling her that she was his and he gets to decide, he took away her power. Then when the monitors didn't immediately step in, they took away the safety of the club."

"Shit" I let out a deep sigh.

"You never felt safe with your mother or in her home, due to both the physical and emotional abuse. Your father consistently showed that you others were more important than you and was never there for you. Actively giving you the fear of abandonment and neglect, both of which occurred during the attack. By hearing all of the events of that night from her, and dealing with the aftermath, your psychological trauma was triggered." I can feel my tears pooling on my blouse. I know she's right but it doesn't make it any easier.

"Kat's attack was a pivotal moment in both of your lives and now journey. It's not something you will ever forget but it is something we can work to get passed. Just like we have before."

Her alarm goes off startling both of us. Handing me a tissue, Jas smiles "Thank you for sharing your story with me today. We will talk again on Thursday, okay?" I sigh loudly "Oh I'm just so looking forward to it." Yeah, my sass is showing, I know it. "Okay, sassy pants, I'll see you in a few days."

Walking out of her office I take what feels like the first deep breath I've taken in months. The hardest part is over. Reliving that was exhausting both physically and mentally. I'm glad I took the rest of the day off. I turn to walk down the street to my favorite coffee shop. After all that I deserve a bit of afternoon caffeine.

CHAPTER 3

LUTHER

*T*his week has been absolute hell and it's only Tuesday. I can't see it getting any better anytime soon either. Owning my own company was always my dream, I wanted to build something that would give me and whoever I chose to spend my life with stability. When I found a need for liquor distribution around the state, I took my chance and Blackout Distributing was born.

What started as a small distributing company, working with small craft breweries and distilleries, has now turned into the third largest distributor in the United States. The last few years though, the world and life seems anything but stable. *Nope, not going there today, I have way too much to get done to fall into that mental clusterfuck.*

Walking the streets of downtown Austin is sweltering in August, but it is the fastest way to get to Cenote, my favorite coffee shop. All my in-person meetings are finally done for the day and I am in major need of a quad espresso. It's only 3:15pm and I've already had to inform four bars, two high-end restaurants, and an event venue that, moving forward, we won't have two of our best selling spirits. They are all upset because it's not going to be available. I'm upset that Adolfo and his daughter Jamie, the owners of HippieHollow Distillers, just lost their family legacy. I'll have to make sure to keep up with them and I will help them anyway I can.

Opening the door to the shop, I'm immediately hit with a blast of cold coffee scented air. There's a short line but it's worth it. Plus, the longer I'm in the air conditioning, the better. Pulling out my phone, I start to check my notifications. From in front of me I hear the most melodic giggle I think I've ever heard. Looking up I see a beautiful young lady, well she's beautiful from behind that's for sure. She has beautiful caramel skin, delicious curves, and her ass in the jeans she's wearing looks absolutely edible.

She's on the phone, and against my better judgment, I let my curiosity get the best of me and listen to her side of the conversation.

"Yeah, I'm okay, it was just a stupid exhausting session, and I'm pretty sure I would do some shady things for some caffeine, at the moment."..."No, I don't think I want to be around anyone tonight. I'm emotionally drained and riding the edge. I think I really just need to decompress and crash out early."..."Yes, I promised I would think about going with you this weekend. I make no promises that I will actually go, though. Look, I gotta go, I'm next."..."Okay, bye boo."

Stepping up to the counter, she orders an extra large triple shot Dulce de leche cheesecake iced macchiato and a cheese danish. The barista asks her if that will be all and that's when she shocks the hell out of me. "Um, yes, please and can I please pay for the next person in line? You can keep the change after!"

As much as I'm impressed, I'm not letting her pay for me, but it does inspire me to do something to give back today.

Quickly speaking up I state, "Excuse me, as much as I appreciate the thought, I can't allow you to pay for my coffee," she whips her head around to look at me so fast, I'm surprised she doesn't get whiplash. I chuckle as I see her face go from shock, to an odd look of awe, to the cutest scowl I think I've ever seen.

Seeing that she's about to argue, I quickly continue, "However, your generosity is wonderful and inspiring." Looking away from her to the barista I say, "Can I get a quad chocolate espresso, please? Also, I would like to instead pay for this lovely Little one's order, as well as anyone else this will cover," pulling out a hundred dollar bill from my wallet.

"Oh, yes, sir," the barista grins at me. The woman who is now standing next to me looks shocked. "Also, this is for y'all's tip jar," I pull a second hundred out of my wallet and place it into the jar.

"Wow! Thank you, sir! Y'all's drinks will be out in just a few minutes."

As we move over to the pick up counter, I notice that she keeps looking back at me, the same scowl on her face. "Why did you do that?" She finally asks.

"Why did I do what?"

"Pay for me when I was trying to pay for you, and then pay for probably everybody else on top of that?" She sounds more confused than actually upset. "I told you, you inspired me," I chuckle, "I promise there was no nefarious reason behind it." I can see she's skeptical but she lets it go with a *humph*.

"I'm Luther, by the way, what's your name?"

"Um, Rose." I smile at her nervousness. "A beautiful name for a beautiful woman." It's then our order is called. "Have a great rest of your day Rose. Keep being a good girl who can inspire others." I watch her eyes widen in pure shock, but don't give her a chance to say anything else, as I walk out of the door.

The rest of the day is spent working with my team to get them looking for a new Tequila, Mezcal, and Pisco distillery. I've always prided myself and my company on working with small family based businesses first. Might not be the least expensive way to conduct business, but the quality is a million times better. I feel horrible that I'm having to look for a new supplier.

Adolfo was the first person to give me a shot as his distributor and now his entire operation has burnt to the ground. I may not have kept a personal relationship with all my contacts but he's different. With that thought in mind I text him to check in:

ME

> How did it go with the Insurance adjuster today?

ADOLFO

> These pendejos are saying that they won't assess damages for payment until the arson investigation is done.

> **ME**
> Sadly, that is standard. So the police confirmed they believe it was arson?

> **ADOLFO**
> Yes, they confirmed it last night. Whatever asshole decided they wanted to burn us down, used gas behind the wheat tank.

> **ME**
> How is Jamie handling everything?

> **ADOLFO**
> Jamie is Jamie...

Shit, I didn't realize they had already determined the fire was arson. That means it's going to take months at minimum for the insurance company to actually work with him. Plus, if I know Jamie, which I do she's going to be freaking out and possibly making herself sick. I'll need to make sure she understands that she and her dad will be just fine.

> **ME**
> Shit! Okay, what do you need from me?

> **ADOLFO**
> Nothing right now. I'm just trying to figure out what's happening next?
>
> Actually, I lied. Get Jamie off my ass. You know you're her favorite anyways.

> **ME**
> I can do that. Don't be mad that your daughter listens to me more than you. At least the brat listens to someone.

> **ADOLFO**
> Yeah yeah 😳

Gathering my stuff, I decide I'm done with work for the day. Hazel eyes float into my mind, Rose. Thinking back on our encounter, I could swear I've seen her before somewhere. That curvy body with an ass I could spend hours worshiping, and a quick witted mouth that I have a feeling, if given a chance, would definitely end up with her over my knee. Shaking off the dirty place my mind is wandering to, I walk to the elevator while texting Jamie.

> **ME**
> Hey Sweet Girl! How are you holding up?

> **JAMIE**
> I'm fine Luther. You know, just trying to figure out how my father is going to survive...

> **ME**
> Come on Little One, you know good and well that your father and you will be fine.

> **JAMIE**
> How L? Everything's gone and now the buttheads from the insurance company are saying we have to wait for the fire investigation.
>
> So until that's all done there's no money and my father is going to end up in financial ruin 😢!!

Oh, so we have our dramatics switched all the way up to high today. Good to know.

> **ME**
> Jams...you know I would never let that happen.

JAMIE
> You won't be able to stop it!! Our lives are over!! Nothing will ever be okay again 😢!

> **ME**
> Jams, I promise it will be okay. I've never lied to you before and I won't start now. Have you had any Jam-Jam time since this all started?

JAMIE
> No and I don't think I'll get to. Honestly I think I'm going to have to give up my membership. With no job I can't afford it anymore.

> **ME**
> I'm going to pretend you didn't just insult me and I'll see you Friday night.

Sighing, I close my phone and head to my car. That Little girl is going to be the death of us all. If she really thinks she's going to lose her membership to a club that I own a percentage of, she's really not thinking. Hell, she only pays a quarter of what everyone else does now anyway and that's only because she insisted and fought us on it. I would never let my favorite Little lose her escape.

I finally let my mind wander to the club. I wouldn't mind

taking the beauty I saw today there. Show her all the ways my mind and body could give her pleasure. Wait a second, I don't even know this woman. When was the last time I let myself indulge? Has it been two months, three maybe? I should play with one of the single subs this weekend and get this pent up sexual energy out. Yeah, I think that's what I'll do. Now the question is, who will I be lucky enough to play with this weekend?

CHAPTER 4

ROSE

*I*t's been two days and I still can't seem to get Luther out of my mind. Work today is slow so I have plenty of time to run through our meeting in my mind again. Not for the first time either. The damned man has been in my dreams two nights in a row now and it's damn annoying. All I can think about is how large his presence was, managing to make me feel small. The dominant way he took over never giving me a chance to say no, going as far as making sure he had the last word. The deviant in me preened and wanted to find a way to push back. I wonder if I will ever see him again.

"Jeez, Rose, pay attention! We only have an hour to finish this schedule before you have to leave. I'm not getting stuck doing it by myself because you are over there daydreaming." Wow, could Carlos be any more dramatic? "It's really not that difficult, you look at what style of car they requested and match it to one that's available. You're acting like it's rocket science."

"Yeah, it may be easy for you, but not all of us work with these cars all day."

Starting to get really irritated and needing to get out some of the 'confrontational energy' I have built up I call over Liliana. "Hey Lili, can I borrow you for a few minutes?"

"Sure! What's up?"

"If I hand you this schedule and this box of keys, what do you do with them?"

Liliana smirks, catching on to what I'm doing. "Go through the list and match the keys to the type of car requested for the pick up. Why?"

I smile, "Oh, just making sure the process wasn't difficult."

"It's not like it's rocket science, Rose. Did you need me to do it and hang the keys up in the lockbox? Should only take me a few minutes." I can tell we have poked the right spot with Carlos. Add in the overly cheerful tone she used and we have him hook, line, and sinker.

"You don't have to do that, Liliana. Rose just wanted to make sure everyone else was up to date on the process before I knock it out." The 'say something and I'll snap' energy that is coming off of him is laughable. He looks like he is ready to explode.

Giggling Lili starts to walk off, calling back, "Okay, I just thought maybe someone couldn't handle basic tasks or something!" That's when I absolutely lose it, laughing like I'm not in the middle of the office. "Let's get this done," Carlos growls.

Just then, I hear my name being called. Looking over, I see Bruce standing at the door to the back offices. Holding up my finger to say one sec, I look at Carlos, "I think you got it, but if it gets too hard go ahead and grab Liliana and she can help you out. I'll let her know."

Smiling, I get up and walk to the back door, feeling damn proud if I do say so myself. "Did you have to be an ass to him?" Bruce chuckles under his breath as we walk to my office.

"Why yes, yes I did. If he would stop being so damn lazy and do his part I wouldn't feel the need to do it." Giving him my best innocent smile, I continue, "Now you called me back here, what's up?"

He shakes his head because he damn well knows better. "You are such a liar, I actually just called you back here so we could review what's needed for tomorrow. Figured you could go to the downtown office, so you can work with and deploy the weekend repo teams. I'll handle things here." Score! I love working at our downtown office, they always have the best snacks, and free energy drinks in the fridge.

"We are having our team meeting at 3pm tomorrow, so it helps you'll already be down there." Matt says, popping his head into the office as he walks past. "It's scary how he does that," I say under my breath. Both me and Bruce chuckle, we both know 'Team Meeting' Really means field trip to the bar next door.

Finalizing the plan for tomorrow doesn't take long and, looking up at the clock, I realize I'm going to need to leave soon if I want to make it to Dr. Jas's on time.

"Alright, I gotta pack up. Leaving in ten," Looking at me with a curious expression Bruce finally asks me what I know he has wanted to for a while. "How has therapy been going?"

Bruce only knows part of what I'm in therapy for, but that's only because he's in the lifestyle, too. I'm pretty sure we are the only ones here who are. "It's going okay. Tuesday was draining and I have a feeling today will be no different," I sigh. "I really hope this part goes by fast. I'm exhausted." He looked at me for just a moment and then smiled. "You'll get there hun, just give yourself time."

Getting in my car, I decide that I need a pick me up before I get there, so I pull up my music app and put my Broadway belting playlist on. Immediately *'Get Down'* from SIX starts playing and I can't help but jam out. Yup, this is exactly what I needed. Pulling into the parking lot I take a deep breath. I know this session is bound to break me. *Sigh.* Let's do this.

"So Rose, our last session was a bit heavy. How have you been doing since?" Apparently, Jas is going to start easy on me today, I'll take it. "It's been okay, work was busy yesterday, so by the time I got home I was in veg-out mode. I did feel openly sassy today, which hasn't happened in a while so there's that."

"Interesting, do you think our last session had anything to do with you getting some sass back?" There's a twinkle in her eye that makes me a little hesitant with my answer, but I decide to be honest with her anyway.

"I'm not sure if it was letting everything out, or if it was an encounter while I was in a fried emotional state. Either way though it was enough to make me be sassy at work today." The smirk that took over her face reminded me of a mom who led her kids to telling them exactly what they needed to know. "Bruce even called me out on it."

Jas flat out laughed at that. "I'm glad you have people in your life that take you for who you really are. Now tell me about this encounter." I start telling her about meeting Luther at the coffee shop, in great detail, leaving nothing out.

"So it seems like maybe his dominance called to your submissive nature. Let me ask you this, have you participated in a scene at all since the incident with Kat?"

"Not really, I haven't really felt it, I guess. Honestly, I haven't even felt sassy. I've been throwing myself into work, and, even there, I've been on really good behavior."

"Why do you think that is?" Gah, I hate it when she does this, like I know you already know the answer, so just tell me. "Okay, so we are playing the throw it back at me game, I see." She just smirks at me and gives me the 'go ahead' nod. "I guess I'm afraid that if I sass the wrong person something bad will happen. Like the protections that are supposed to be there will fail again."

Jas nods. "What about Harrison? He has been your primary play partner for over a year, and y'all have been friends for years right?" She genuinely looks curious.

"Yeah, we have been friends for almost ten years, I don't think it has anything to do with him why we haven't scened in months. Heck, he has been trying to get me to go to the club with him for weeks now. Says he thinks it might help if I go, even if it's just to hang out, watch maybe. I just don't know, what if something happens?"

Jas pauses and looks like she's thinking deeply about what I just laid out to her. After a minute she takes a deep breath and looks at me with a serious look on her face. "Honestly, I think Harrison might have the right idea here. The night of

Kat's assault you lost your trust in your community and the people around you. We've talked before about how the reason you trusted Harrison with your body was because he is always careful with your mind. I think he is the perfect person for you to take this step with. Go and just spend time at F.O.U.R.S, get reacclimated with the environment. You don't have to participate, but by being there to observe and seeing the system you thought was in place, in action, I truly believe you might be able to get past some of the trauma. Maybe even be able to let your submissive side out."

"Well, that's not something I ever thought I would hear coming from you," I say sarcastically.

"What part is that?" She says with a giggle.

"The 'I agree with Harrison' part," I say with a sigh. "Alright, I'll agree to go, I'll text him when I leave here."

Just then the timer goes off, "And just like that we are at time. I just want to remind you that starting next week we are going back down to one session a week. So I'll see you on Wednesday."

Jas stands up to walk me out and I do something I haven't done in months, I hug her. "Thank you Jas, I don't know what I would do without you." With that I leave her office.

CHAPTER 5

ROSE

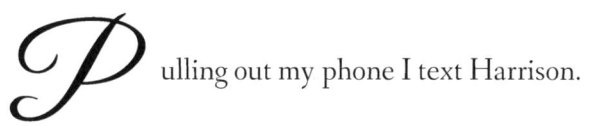

*P*ulling out my phone I text Harrison.

HARRISON

So have you thought anymore about going to the club with me Friday? I really think it'll be good for you!! Plus we always have fun 😊!

ME

I really don't know yet... I promise I'll let you know soon.

Well hell has frozen over and Jas actually agrees with you. I guess I'm going to the club with you tomorrow. I don't think I'll play tho.

HARRISON

FUCK YES I'LL TAKE IT!

Been telling you for years I'm a genius! Wear something hot as shit for me! I'll pick you up at 9.

> Actually, I'll just come over early!

> Shut up oh excited one...I'll see you tomorrow. I'll be home by 6:30. — ME

There's no backing out now......

CHAPTER 6

ROSE

Today has been exhausting. Why men in the car industry think us women in the car industry are stupid, I will never know. Add in the misogynistic comments and you have a recipe for a pissed off Rose souffle. I am more than ready to head out when Matt and Bruce walk into the office. "You're late," I quipped, giving them a scathing look.

"Well somebody is feeling a bit grumpy," Matt looked shocked when he heard my sassy, overly tired tone. "Everything okay?"

"No, I've been dealing with assholes all day. I'm not sure there is enough caffeine in this building to pull me out of the energy drain vortex I'm in." Shaking his head at me Matt waves me over so we can head out.

It only takes a few minutes to get to our favorite bar. It helps that it's just next door. Matt and I immediately head out back to our favorite table while Bruce grabs drinks. "So tell me what has you in attack mode this afternoon," Matt asks as soon as we sit down.

"Same shit different day, I seriously think we need to use a different towing company. Chauvinistic pigs towing just isn't it." Matt explodes with laughter. "I like that. I might have to change their name in my phone. I told you I can take over dealing with them so you don't have to."

I give him my best 'don't try me' look, "And I told you that I'm not handing it over just because they can't handle the fact that they answer to a woman." He quickly puts his hands in the air in the universal 'letting it go' gesture and winks at me.

Bruce walks up right as he does and laughs, "Rose what did you do to the boss man now? His face is screaming 'don't shoot'."

"Oh, you know just having the same jerks of towing conversation as always. Ummm, Bruce you were only going for beers for you two and cider for me. Why the hell do you have shots? And why do you look like the cat who ate the canary?"

"I figured you needed a little something to take the edge off. Don't worry it's just one," sliding over my cider and the glass. "And it's tequila. I remembered."

Sighing, I clink my glass with the guys shots of whiskey and take my shot. Wow, he really had remembered, I thought as the smooth flavor of Hippiehollow Blanco slid down my throat warming me from the inside. "Let's get the work talk out of the way so we can chill."

The door to our apartment feels like a portal. As I cross the threshold, I can feel just how mentally exhausted I truly am from this cluster fuck rollercoaster of a week. With the anxiety of Kat coming home in just two days, and the tidal wave of emotions that therapy has brought up; on top of the normal daily stress of work and life, has me yearning to just let go. I'm just hoping I can manage it tonight. I know I'm safe with Harrison and he wouldn't let anything happen to me, but the idea of being back in a club environment has me feeling on edge.

Setting my bag down on the living room table, I pull out my phone to text Harrison. I might be in knots but I'm going to see this through.

ME
Hey, I'm home now.

HARRISON
Oh awesome. You're home a lot earlier than you said. I'm running an errand and then I'll be over there. Do you need anything?

ME
Ummmmm... A sedative and a large drink?

HARRISON
Oh BooBear...I'll be there soon.

Knowing Harrison will probably be a while, I decide to make sure I'm ready for anything tonight. I grab a cider from the fridge and head into the bathroom. Turning on the shower to let it have time to heat up, I connect my phone to the shower speaker and plug it in to the charger we keep in here. Hitting the shuffle button on my 'Naughty Night Out' playlist the upbeat sounds of Lost in Paradise start playing. Swaying my hips I remove my clothes, throw them in the hamper and grab my exfoliation basket from the closet. Stepping in the shower, I let the hot water sting my skin, starting a routine I know all too well.

Forty minutes later I've managed to shave and exfoliate every inch of my body. I get out and dry off, having finished off my cider, I head to the kitchen to grab myself another and let the steam in the bathroom dissipate.

Heading back to the bathroom I hear the rhythmic knocking at my door. Only one person knocks like they are playing the drums so I don't even bother looking through the peephole. Hiding behind the door since I'm just in a towel, I let Harrison in.

"Did you even look to see who it was?" The look he's giving me tells me he already knows the answer. Knowing there's no point in lying to him, I give him the truth. "There was no need, it's not like I didn't know it was you, no one else knocks like that."

"That's not the point Rose, just because you know how I knock doesn't mean someone couldn't copy it to get to you. You always need to check first," rolling my eyes, I start to walk away from him, taking a sip of my drink.

"Whatever you say, big man." A large hand wraps around my waist from behind, "I see we are feeling sassy tonight. Do you need a reminder of who is in charge here this early on?" I stop and really think about my answer before I give it, "Not really, what I need is to moisturize before my pores close up and fix my hair before it dries. I just got out of the shower, Harrison." It takes a minute for Harrison to loosen his hold on me. I start to walk back to the bathroom when he finally speaks again. "Finish up and then we are going to talk about tonight," flashing him a pensive look, I nod.

I'm standing in the mirror putting the final touches on my make-up sans lip, when Harrison walks up and leans on the doorframe. "How are we doing in here?" I look over at him and I know he can see the trepidation in my eyes. "I'm okay, I guess," even I can hear the insincerity in my voice.

Giving me 'the look', he leans even further into the doorframe. "We have been friends for a decade and play partners for I don't know how long, if you think I can't read you as easily as a picture book, we really need to reevaluate both dynamics. Now, tell me how you're really doing."

I take a deep breath to try and keep in the overwhelming feeling of wanting to cry. I just did my make up dammit, I have to give the waterproof mascara time to dry. "Honestly?" Harrison nods. "I don't fully know how to comprehend how I'm feeling. I know you will always take care of me and that I can trust you. I know you won't let anyone hurt me, but my brain is in a talespin. I'm overwhelmed, scared, excited, confused, eager,…it's like all of these feelings are going round and round in my head and I can't seem to get them under control. I don't know what to do, or how to handle this," I know my voice is getting louder and I can feel the panic taking over my ability to breathe. Looking up, I gasp "Harrison please," and just like that he scoops me up and carries me to the living room.

Sitting on the couch with me in his lap, Harrison grabs my chin in a tight grip and turns me to look at him. "Okay Sweetheart, breathe with me," using his free hand he places my hand on his chest, "in and out." I follow his lead breathing with him. "That's it," another deep breath, "that's my good girl." We sit there for a few more minutes just breathing together. When I'm finally calm again Harrison breaks the silence.

"Okay Sweetheart, here's how I think we should handle tonight. As usual, I will be your Sir tonight, but instead of us starting at the club, like we usually do, we are going to start here. Unless you are opposed to it, I will take over from here, that way you don't need to make any more decisions, and we can get you partially settled in sub space before we get to the club. How does that sound?" I don't even have to hesitate, "Yes, Sir, please."

Helping me stand, Harrison turns me in his arms, "How much have you had to drink this evening?" I chuckle "One cider and a shot of tequila at the bar, and one full cider since I got home, plus whatever is gone out of the one on the bathroom counter."

Satisfied with my answer he smirks, "Good, Sweetheart. Now here's what you are going to do, you are going to go into your room, bend over the bed with a pillow under your hips, and extend your arms over your head. Wait for me in that position and I will be there in just a moment." The dark deep tone that his voice has taken sends shivers down my spine. There is both the promise of pleasure and the threat of punishment in that tone and I love it.

Walking to my room I could feel myself giving over to his dominance. I'm too tired to fight it right now. Attacks like the one I just had always take it out of me. Walking up to my bed I grab my fluffiest pillow and bend over like he asked. It wasn't long before I heard him moving behind me, his dark chuckle giving away his location. "Tsk, Tsk, Rose, you're still wearing your robe, that wasn't what I asked of you," smirking because I know he can't see me I respond. "You told me to come in and bend over the bed with a pillow, you gave no instructions when it came to my robe, Sir." I knew it was cheeky and that he had wanted me bare when he came in, but I couldn't help the small defiance, it was too easy.

I hear Harrison walking up behind me, then I feel his hand on my rear. "I sure do love it when you're defiant, gives me reason to turn this ass a pretty shade of red. I'm going to enjoy this." A shiver runs up my spine knowing that spanking is his favorite form of punishment and I'm about to get a glorious one. "For being defiant, I am going to give you five, and for not telling me you needed me to be in charge from the beginning, I am going to give you another five. These are on top of what I already had planned for you. Do you understand?"

My breath catches, not at the thought of the spanking but at what is to come after. "Umm, yes Sir," I know he can hear the hesitance in my voice. "Do you trust me Rose?"

I realize quickly my hesitance might make him question if I'm truly here with him. "Yes Sir, I was just thinking about your additional plans." I hear him release the breath he was holding, "Good girl, let me take care of you tonight sweet girl. Tomorrow you can go back to being your badass self. Now Sweets, what's your safe word?"

I don't hesitate, "Pothos, Sir." I can hear the smile in his voice, "Good girl, don't worry about counting for these. This is going to be fast and hard," and with that, he begins.

Somewhere around smack seven I felt myself beginning to separate from the physical sting caused by his palm and start feeling the floating feeling that giving over to submission always provides. By ten, I was hovering right above the cloud. I can't help but think, *This, this is what I needed.* Harrison knows me. *I can trust him, he won't let things get out of hand. I am safe.*

"You've done so well, Sweetheart." I hear the click of a bottle. "Now, I am going to insert this small plug, it is only there to remind you that I am with you at all times tonight, do you understand?"

The jerk is prepping me while asking me a question, rude much? "Yes, Sir. I understand." I feel the small toy sliding in, he wasn't lying, it is tiny. Tapping my hip Harrison gives me the okay to sit up and turn around. "Now Sweetheart, have you chosen your outfit for tonight?"

I look down at my hands and start playing with the ring I always have on my middle finger. "No, Sir, I didn't have an idea of what I wanted to wear, so I figured I would get ready first and then go from there."

Harrison places his finger under my chin and raises my face to look at him. "That's okay, go fix your make-up and finish getting the rest of you ready. I will handle clothing, meet me in the living room when you're ready." I nod and start to walk back towards the bathroom, "Oh and Rose, wear the blood red lipstick, it will look the best."

CHAPTER 7

ROSE

It's almost 9:30 by the time Harrison and I go to leave the house. As we step into the rideshare, I'm feeling absolutely beautiful. Harrison surprised me with a new sexy royal purple dress and gorgeous matching lingerie set for tonight. I don't know if anybody will actually see the set, but just knowing that it's there makes me feel fantastic.

The ride to the club doesn't usually take very long, but today it feels like it takes three times longer. Even being partially in subspace, my emotions still feel like they are speeding down a highway. As we pull up in front of the club, Harrison grabs my hand, "It's gonna be okay, Sweetheart. I've got you. Remember that okay."

Stepping out of the rideshare I can't stop my racing thoughts. *I know it's time. I have to face my fears. What if something happens? No, you can do this. Harrison's got you.* Harrison squeezes my hand and I know it's time.

Looking at the club from the street, you would never guess that a BDSM club lay within the unassuming building.

Bold white lettering hangs on the wall next to the matte black door. I absolutely adore the speakeasy warehouse vibe.

Harrison opens the door and immediately my anxiety starts to spike. I have to stop and take a deep breath before I step. The familiar scent of warm vanilla and mint fill my lungs and for the first time this evening I feel like I can breathe.

Walking towards the ornate front desk, I smile and wave at Laura and Dante. The receptionist and security guard standing next to the door have been here for as long as I've been coming. "Hey, Rose! Harrison! It feels like it's been forever since we last saw you! How have you been?"

I can't help the cheesy smile that crosses my face, Laura is always so sweet and a huge ball of energy. "Yeah, it has been quite a while, I've had to deal with some stuff. How are you two?" I swear the woman in front of me is bouncing like she's had an entire gallon of ice cream today. "We have been soooo good. The club has gotten busier since the gross one across town was forced to shut down. That's okay though because I hear they weren't very nice over there and they..."

Dante must have seen the way my face started to pale when Laura brought up Peaks. I know Harrison could feel me lock up. Dante's deep timber cuts in before Laura can continue. "What Laura here was trying to say is we've been good and the club is booming." Looking away from us, Dante gives Laura a look that even I understand as 'let it go, now'. He continues, "Why don't you get them checked in, cupcake. I'm sure they are anxious to get on with their night."

Looking shocked, like the thought never even crossed her mind Laura skipped over to the computer, "OH MY GOOD-

NESS YES! Let's get you guys checked in! I'm so sorry, sometimes my brain runs away with my mouth."

I can't help the giggle that slips out of me. Even Harrison is giggling at the sprite of a woman. Before I can get out another word Harrison speaks up, "That's alright Little one, but Dante is right, we would love to get inside. I think Rose here could use a drink."

Pointing down at the thumb reader, Laura lets the smile engulf her face again. "Well, let's not dilly dally then! Go ahead and scan in." We do as she continues, "okay so are we sticking with the gold level bands tonight or are we switching things up?"

Immediately I look down at my wrist and the gold level membership band that we are both wearing sits around my wrist and then turn to look at Harrison. We've always used the gold bands, so I don't know what else we would get. "We are still using the gold bands, but can you add a black charm to Rose's for tonight?"

I look over at Harrison confused, "Of course! I'll be right back with that!" Laura squeaks. Harrison finally looks over at me with a smirk. "What's the black bead for?" I ask, "Really Rose, has it been that long since you've been here?"

I roll my eyes at him, "I know what the bead means Harrison, but what I'm wondering is why you're adding it tonight." Harrison adopts a stern expression, "First of all, this is your one and only warning while we are here. Second, I am adding a black charm because you are already anxious about tonight. This way if any other Dominants would like to approach you, they know that they have to go through me first. While generally most Dominants will recognize your partner band as a sign they should go through your partner first, it is a common courtesy not a rule. This way every Dominant in this building knows that, at least for tonight, you are not to be approached without my permission."

I can't help but look at Harrison with wonder. I never even thought about that. The deep rumble that comes from my left pulls me from my frozen state, unable to hold his laugh in any longer, Dante lets go. I give him my best 'that's so rude' look and it does absolutely nothing to stop his laugh. "I'm sorry Rose. I just love it when people get the full blown 'They really do have my best interest in mind' look. Yours was absolutely comical."

Pouting, I look up at Harrison, "I didn't have a look, did I?" But the answer didn't come from Harrison, "Oh, you totes had that look. I do it all the time to this big Meanybutt." A low growl comes from Dante at Laura's comment. "Any whose! Let me see your wrist Rose and we will get you two a movin!"

Unhooking my band, which is really more a bracelet anyway, Laura slides on the black charm and locks it to the other two already there. Green for open to others and silver for Submissive. While Laura works on my band Harrison steps over to Dante for his security check. The security and safety measures here are one of the things I love about coming to F.O.U.R.S. I can't help feeling a little more at ease. *What happened at Peaks would never be allowed here. I'm safe.* Before I know it Laura's placing my band back on my wrist and we are good to go. Stepping over to Dante, I hand him my bag to look over. He quickly looks through the meager contents and hands it back with a smile, "y'all have fun tonight." I let loose a huge smile when Laura chirps, "have so, so, soooo, much fun!" Having seen the way Dante looked at her I just giggled.

Harrison grabs my hand and we start through the door. Before it closes all the way, I catch Dante's words to Laura, "I'm a Meanybutt, am I, Cupcake?" At hearing that, I let out a full blown laugh, helping me relax even more.

CHAPTER 8

LUTHER

The club is busy tonight and that fills my heart with joy. When we opened this club, we were all worried that it would never take off. Texas is extremely conservative, even here in Austin, which is a pretty accepting area.

As I walk through the club I'm stopped multiple times by long term members that want to greet me or introduce me to their visitors. When I finally make it to the bar, I am more than ready for a drink. I make eye contact with Miranda, our bartender and wave. She's with another customer, but I know she saw me. Turning to make their drinks, Miranda looks over and mouths, 'usual'? I give a swift nod and turn to eye the crowd.

I love this time of the night, being just shy of ten, most of the patrons still in the lounge are long time members. They know just how enticing the anticipation of what is to come can be. The newer and younger members usually get here early and don't mingle long, wanting to get their fun started as fast as possible. As I'm scanning the main floor, my attention is caught by the most melodic sound I think I've ever heard. When I look at the entrance door, I can't believe my eyes. It's the girl from the coffee shop, she's here. How did I get this lucky?

She looks stunning in a dress that fits her voluptuous body perfectly. Holding hands with Harrison, a long time member and friend of mine, they make their way to the couch area on the side of the lounge. I feel a small tap on my wrist and a tumbler appears next to it. Picking up my Tequila Blanco on the rocks I smirk at Miranda. "Thank you, dear. How is your night going so far?"

Scoffing at my blatant fake flirting, "It's been fine, but I could really use another bartender back here. I know Aire can only work Monday-Wednesday, and I fully support her being a badass superhero mom and student, but weekends have become torture."

This is the first time I've heard anything about this. "What's got it feeling that way?" Miranda looks a bit hesitant so I give her the best reassurance I can. "Miranda, you have been our lead bartender for two years, you have a perfect track record and I trust you implicitly. Now, what's going on?"

Sighing heavily she starts, "Please don't be mad at me okay...as much as that other club closing has been great for our business, and it really has, it has brought a ton of extra members in. I'm just one person, Luther. I'm running back and forth all night long to serve drinks, and if that isn't exhausting enough, I'm constantly having to find someone to grab things from the back for me since the last bar back quit.

By the time my shift is over on Sunday, I'm dead. I've been making it work but it's not sustainable."

I take a moment to let her words sink in. I glance around the bar, seeing the line forming and feel a rock sink in my stomach. Looking where I'm looking she sighs heavily, "I gotta go boss. Thanks for letting me vent." Before she can walk away I say, "Let me know what you need by your shift on Thursday. I know you're gonna be too busy this weekend to even try to think it through, but I want to know." She gives me a smile and wanders back to her line.

Grabbing my drink off the bar, I turn to scan the crowd in the lounge. Subconsciously, I know I'm looking for the girl that has taken residence in my brain. Half way through my scan I spot her. She and Harrison have taken a spot on the couch set in the corner of the room. I don't want to come on too strong, so I decide I will walk the floor and 'bump' into them.

As I'm walking I spot Allie, one of our most energetic servers coming out of the back staff area. "Hey, Allie," I say with a smile on my face. "Hey, Boss Man! What's up?" I love how comfortable the staff is with me. I may mainly deal with the paperwork side of the business, but I make it a point to get to know our staff.

"Did you just get in?" I ask her. "Yes Sir, did you need some help?" I can't help but chuckle at her slightly flirty tone. "Actually, I do." giving her my thousand watt smile, I make my request, "I know you used to bartend before you started here, so I was wondering if you would be willing to help Miranda out this weekend. I will gladly make sure you are compensated appropriately since you are coded as a server."

She pauses, thinking about my offer, "I can do that this weekend, sir and I don't mind helping out." I can see the BUT from a mile away, "but if it's okay with you I would like to stay a server on a regular basis. The tips are fantastic and I really need the flexibility."

I can't help but smirk, "Of course you can, she just needs some help this weekend and maybe next. If you can't next weekend, that's okay, I can ask one of the other girls later." She beams up at me, "Thank you so much for understanding, sir! I don't mind helping out this weekend and next. Really it's no problem, y'all have always taken care of me," and with that she skips off to the bar to help Miranda.

Getting closer to the table Harrison and Rose are sitting at I notice that she seems tense. Her body is rigid and she's got what looks like a death grip on Harrison's hand. She looks almost scared to be here. That won't do, that just won't do at all. I know Harrison would never do anything to put someone on alert the way she is, so what has her feeling this way?

I look down to their wrists and notice she has a black charm. While it does ease my mind that Harrison is here as her partner, and she is most likely clinging to him for comfort, it does not bode well for me to be able to ask her what's wrong.

Stepping up to the table, I greet Harrison. "Harrison, good to see you." I see her eyes shoot up at the sound of my voice, the look of pure shock on her face would be comical if I didn't already sense something was off.

Harrison rises to shake my hand. "Luther, I didn't know you would be in tonight. Join us for a drink, yeah?" He looks down at Rose to make sure she's okay with me joining and she gives a small nod. I try to ignore the unwarranted jealousy bubbling up from their obvious connection. "Thanks, I would love to," I say, smiling at the couple as I sit down.

Since I'm not able to speak to Rose directly until Harrison gives permission, I direct my inquiries towards him. "I didn't know you and Rose here were an item. Actually, I didn't know you were involved with anyone at all." He gives a low chuckle under his breath before sending a quizzical smile down at Rose. "Well, that's because at least in the traditional sense, we aren't involved. We are both single. Rose and I have been play partners for a while now and have been best friends even longer. How do you two know each other?"

The relief I feel at his explanation of their relationship is unexpected. I still feel the burning sensation of jealousy, but it's lessened now that I know she isn't officially taken. Realizing I've frozen and haven't answered Harrison's question yet, I clear my throat. "We actually met earlier this week, had a run in at the coffee shop," I give them both a wicked smirk. "It was...an energizing encounter to say the least." That has Rose chuckling, I could bathe in that sound.

The recognition on Harrison's face says he knows exactly the encounter I'm talking about. With shock in his voice, he turns his face to Rose, "You didn't tell me Luther was the guy from the coffee shop." Rose gives him a confused look before she responds, "Sir, I didn't know that you two knew each other," her voice is low and slightly apologetic. Before she continues she casts her eyes downward, "had I known, I would have told you."

The submissive tone and body language she is using causes a tugging in my groin. What I would give to have that beautiful submission aimed towards me. Harrison places his finger under her chin and lifts her eyes to his. He strokes her cheek with one of his other fingers, staring directly into her eyes, he tells her, "Sweetheart, it is okay, you had no way of knowing that we knew each other. I could never be upset with you for something you had no idea about. I was surprised, that's all. I've known Luther for a few years now. We met when I started the designs for F.O.U.R.S. He's one of the owners."

I don't think she expected his answer and I can't help but chuckle at the astounded look that crosses her face. Leaning over she whispers something in Harrison's ear. When he pulls back, he smiles and nods. I can physically see her relax at his answer. Whatever she asked must have been important.

She leans back in, a sparkle in her beautiful hazel eyes and whispers something else. When she's done, he leans back on the couch with a chuckle. "Of course, Sweetheart, you may have permission to speak to Luther directly." With a shy smile to Harrison she responds, "Thank you, Sir."

Turning to me, I can see the hesitance in her eyes. I try to give her the most reassuring smile I can. "Even though it's a shock, it's nice to see you again Luther." My name coming from her lips...nothing has ever felt so right.

CHAPTER 9

ROSE

He's here...how is Luther here? I know my anxiety can make me feel some crazy things, but it's never made me hallucinate. Listening to Luther and Harrison talk is surreal. They know each other? He owns the club?!?!?! I need to breathe before I pass out...my anxiety hasn't calmed down much since we got here. Not even knowing I'm safe with Harrison and that no one can approach me or even talk to me, without his permission, has been able to calm the pin prick feeling crawling through me from my fingers to my toes. I lean over and whisper in Harrison's ear, "Is he safe, can I trust him?" When he nods at me a little of my anxiety falls away, leaning back in I take a leap of faith.

"Even though it's a shock, it's nice to see you again Luther." My tone sounds a bit sassy even to my ears. Harrison chuckles to my right, but I can't focus on that right now.

Luther's eyes are alight with fire, and his full lips have a

BREATHE

sexy side smirk that makes a whole new type of tingle start within my body. "Believe me, Sweetheart, the pleasure is all mine." Luther's low growly tone wraps around me like a warm blanket on a cold day. I can't help but lean forward towards the absolute force of a man that's in front of me. *How is it that eight little words, from a man I've met all of one time, can make me feel secure in a situation?* "So tell me more about yourself mister..." I let my voice trail letting him know I want him to fill in his last name. Luther chuckles, "Breedlove, Luther Breedlove." *Hmmm, I like that name.* "Well, Mr. Breedlove, tell me about yourself...."

LUTHER

I love the sound of this woman's voice. "Well, thanks to Harrison here, you already know that I am a part owner here, but this is not my day to day. I work in distribution." The absolute confusion on her face when I said that was adorable. In a whisper she asks "Um, when you say distribution...is it legal?"

Harrison howls with laughter from his seat on the couch and I can't help but laugh, too. "Oh, Sweetheart," Harrison gasps out through his laughter, "do you really think I would work with someone in that line of business?" I watch the heat of embarrassment crawl across her olive skin and see the flash of heated sass in her eyes.

Before she can get herself in trouble I respond, "Yes, babygirl, it's legal. I own a liquor distribution company, nothing nefarious." She gives me a grin that I can only call mischievous. "What does your girlfriend think about you owning two such businesses?" Ah, so we are digging I see, "I don't have a girlfriend, babygirl. If I did, I wouldn't even consider entertaining another woman. When I am with a woman, she is mine. Mind, body, and soul."

I see fire ignite behind her eyes, "So you're a possessive man?" I smirk, "I take care of who and what is mine. No matter what that entails. I wouldn't say I'm possessive per se, but I am protective. Sharing in the club is one thing, as long as all parties agree. Sharing outside, well I can honestly say that's not something I have ever entertained."

I swear I can see the embers shining in her eyes. Her breathing is getting slightly shallower and there are goosebumps running down her arms. "Now let's get back to the task at hand. Getting to know each other." Harrison is trying to hold back his laughter. "What do you do for a living?" I can see the whiplash my question caused her and it's adorable.

"Um I-Im a Fleet coordinating assistant for the central Texas branch of CarryYouThere. Basically, I help keep that part of the business's wheels turning. No pun intended." I can't help but smile at her small stutter. "CarryYouThere as in the rideshare company?" I ask. "Ye-P" She says, popping the P.

"Interesting, I wasn't aware that they had a rental car program. How do you like it?" She pauses to take a moment to think about it and I appreciate that. "My job can be really stressful sometimes since there are only three of us on my side of things, but I adore my coworkers. Well, at least most of them. Plus, getting to help people have a way to work that wouldn't usually be able to drive rideshare because of their car or lack thereof is super rewarding."

I naturally smile at that. This night has definitely taken a turn for the better. I can't help my smirk, "So tell me Rose, what do you do to relieve stress?" The nervous giggle she lets out tells me I've got her.

HARRISON

I'm sitting back listening to the two of them and can't keep my smile off my face. I've always loved the sound of this woman's laugh and it's been absent lately. I've tried my hardest to care for her, but I always knew it wasn't enough. Do we play together? Yes. Is she one of my best friends? Absolutely. Am I the right man for her? Not at all.

The immediate connection she has with Luther is undeniable. Watching them together, it's almost like they have their own orbit and I'm just lucky enough to fit inside. "So tell me Rose, what do you do to relieve stress?" The smirk Luther gives her when he asks that question can only be described as sultry. Hell, I'm even a little flustered.

"Well, I love to read," Rose has the most adorable look on her face. I can tell she's nervous about moving anything forward tonight, I rub my thumb on her back to remind her I'm here. "I also love plants. I wish I could have an actual garden, but we live in an apartment." I can't help but chuckle. That's not what he meant and she knows it. I can tell by the look on his face that Luther can see it, too. She's being obtuse on purpose, so I decide to push her a bit.

"She also loves to sass till her ass is grass." Rose whips her head around at me to give me a smoldering glare. "Sir, you love my sassy mouth, and it's not my fault you like to test how long it takes to turn my ass red. So, I mean this with all due respect, BITE ME." She immediately turns away from me to look back at Luther, almost smacking me in the face with her curls. I sit up and lean over her shoulder.

The best part about the dress I got her is the access I have to her shoulders and neck. Bending down just a bit, I bite down on the sweet spot where her neck meets her shoulder. The moan she lets out is carnal. "Sir," she whimpers, all it does is make me bite a little harder. "Sir, please, that's not fair."

I release her neck and give it a small lick to ease the sting. "I was just giving you what you asked for, Sweetheart. Don't ask for things you aren't ready for, because you know I'll follow through. EVERY. SINGLE. TIME." I drove those last words home with nips between them. I can see the goosebumps running down her arms, and feel her heart racing.

I lean back in my seat trying to ignore my now raging erection. I continue rubbing Rose's back to anchor her. Looking over at Luther, I can't help but notice his pants seem a bit tighter as well. I might be wrong, but it seems that he isn't just looking at Rose, but looking at me too.

"So you like biting, do you?" I can't tell if that statement is directed at me or Rose, and she is still in a flustered state so I answer. "She loves it, and so do I. The taste of her skin is on par with heaven. Plus the noises she makes...delicious." I watch Luther's eyes darken as I speak, he's looking at me like he wants to take a bite out of me. *Why is the way he's looking at me setting my blood on fire?* I can't lie and say I've never thought of being with a man, but I've never explored that side of myself.

I break the eye contact we have somehow gotten stuck in and look over at Rose, "How are you doin', Sweetheart? Can you give me a color check-in?" I need to make sure she's still okay with how things are moving. She is my number one priority tonight. Smiling over at me replying, "green, Sir." Her voice is breathy and her cheeks are hot. "Good Girl." I look back over at Luther and give him a small nod letting him know he can continue. This night looks like it might be more interesting than I thought.

CHAPTER 10

ROSE

It's getting hotter by the second, I reach down to pick up my drink just to find it empty. I can feel the pout take over my face as soon as that realization hits me. "Would you like another drink, sweet girl?" The smile on Luther's face as Harrison asks me makes my heart warm. "Yes, Sir. Can I please have a tequila and redbull?" I ask with a flutter of my eyes.

"Sure, Sweetheart." With that Harrison goes to rise, but Luther waves him back down. "Don't worry about it, I'll go grab them. Do you want anything Harrison?" Harrison gives him his order and Luther walks to the bar.

Harrison turns to face me fully, "Next move is yours, Sweetheart. Do you want to stay out here or move into the club? Remember, I am okay with whatever you want to do." I can feel my heart rate increase at the idea of going into the play area of the club. I scan the room and see Luther staring at us from where he stands by the bar. Our eyes lock and a sense of warm calm rushes over me.

Without looking over to Harrison, I let my mouth say what my heart was screaming, "I think I want to go into the club, Sir. I think I-I'm good with that. I don't know about anyone else touching me, but I think I want to explore." I turn and look into Harrison's eyes. There's adoration there along with lust. "Why don't we take it slow and, after our drinks, we visit the voyeur lounge? That way you can watch...and we can watch you." I notice at the word 'we' Harrison's pupils blew wide. *Well, there's something to unpack later.*

It doesn't take long for Luther to come back with our drinks. "Why do I feel like you two are over here plotting?" He asks with a devilish grin. Both me and Harrison giggle, but I shoot back easily, "Because we were, we can't bring you to your knees without a little planning first." Both men's faces looked shocked at my quick and sassy retort.

"Well, it looks like someone found their boldness while I was gone." The hunger in Luther's eyes tells me he's more than comfortable with this change of events, but just to make sure I ask, "does that bother you, Mr. Breedlove?" The look he sends me sends magma through my veins.

His normally slight accent is thick as gravy when he answers, "no Darlin', nothin' would make me happier than to hear bold sassiness come from your mouth. Just know I may handle your sassy mouth a bit differently than Harrison would." My mouth hangs open at his response, and he just chuckles. "Careful there, Darlin', you never know what could find its way in there. Now, you wanna fill me in on your plot?"

I'm still stuck on his last comment so I just look to Harrison to help. Just like I knew he would, he comes to my rescue, "The plan is to head into the voyeur room after we finish these drinks, since no alcohol is allowed back there. Would you care to join us or do you have other plans?"

My brain is still stuck so I finally just spit it out "WAIT! WAIT! WAIT! What do you mean the way you would handle it would be different?" Harrison grabs my hand, noticing my anxiety was taking over, "Sweetheart, it's okay, he didn't mean anything bad by it." Glaring at him I snap, "Well then, what the hell DID he mean?"

Harrison gives me a look that tells me I'm going to be in trouble for that little snap, but before he can say anything Luther speaks up. "It means that I'm a Daddy Dom, Darlin'. The way I handle sassiness doesn't always match the way other Doms do. That's all Darlin'. Now, is that anyway to speak to your Sir?" *Well, shit...*

My voice comes out breathier than I expected, "no Sir, it isn't." I turn to Harrison, "I'm sorry, Sir. Snapping at you was rude."

Harrison nods at me and looks at my drink. "Sweetheart, it looks like we need to address a few things before we can enjoy our night further. I've let multiple things slide, so far," I can feel my ass starting to tingle with every word that he speaks. When he goes to stand I can't help but look at him confused. "I'll be right back, Sweetheart." I watch him walk up to the club's concierge and say something. The delighted smirk that comes over the concierge's face does not help.

The deep chuckle from across the table brings my focus back to Luther. "Looks like you've earned yourself a punishment, Darlin'. Are you alright with me staying or would you like me to leave?" *Did he really just ask me that?* "I thought it was a given that if you were receiving a public punishment, anyone around could view?" I ask.

"Technically, yes, but I will always do what makes you the most comfortable. Sweet Darlin', it's important to remember, you are the one who always has the ultimate control." It's then that I knew I could trust him. Only a real Dom would ask questions like that, or remind you that ultimately as the submissive you really have the control. "Stay, Luther, please?" I finally ask. "Of course, Darlin', I'll be here."

CHAPTER 11

HARRISON

The walk from the table to the concierge isn't far, but it does give me time to decide just how I want to handle Rose's outburst. I knew she would push tonight, it's a given when she's feeling anxious. What I didn't expect was her connection with Luther, or her feeling comfortable enough to not just push, but to be full on sassy.

Smiling as I get to the concierge, I let him know what I need and give him my last name so he can put it into the system. I can't help but look at them while I wait for him to return. They look good together. I'm surprised that Rose wants to play in any capacity tonight, especially with how she was feeling leading up to us even coming to the club. We shall see how she feels after her punishment, but I think my girl might be more ready than even I thought.

The concierge walks back and hands me a basket full of the equipment I requested. I look over everything to make sure I have what I need and nod. With a thanks, I turn and head back to the table. As I near, I watch the way Luther looks at Rose. It's like she's the only one in the room. I don't think he has even noticed me walking up yet.

"Stay, Luther, please?" I hear her ask. "Of course, Darlin', I'll be here." It's then he looks up and sees me walking up. The carnal look he throws my way has my blood heating even further. *Why does that do so much to me? Am I into Luther? It doesn't matter either way because he's straight. Why am I even thinking about this right now? I need to focus, Rose is my priority.*

"Ah, Harrsion, looks like you've found some goodies there." *Damn is Luther's accent getting even thicker?* "Oh, I have. I think Rose here needs a reminder on how she should address her Sir," I sit down before I continue, "Sweetheart, stand up for me." Rose takes a deep breath and rises to her feet turning to face me.

My poor girl is even more nervous than normal. I take a deep breath, too, and I look her in the eye. "Okay Sweets, here's what's going to happen. You are going to come here and bend over my knee. I will be switching out your plug and adding a little something extra. Then you will count out while I spank that already tender ass five times."

She looks shocked that I only said five but I keep going, "you are not allowed to cum. Do you understand why you are being punished and do you agree with it?" She nods her head slowly, "Yes, Sir. I was disrespectful and I deserve to be punished." The contrite look on her face and the response eases my worries about punishing her tonight.

There's just a few more things we need to review, "You are only getting five swats this time because I know your outburst came from shock more than you actually trying to be a brat. Can you confirm your color for me, Sweets?" She pauses a bit longer than I would like, but then finally says, "Honestly, I'm some weird mix between green and yellow, Sir."

She looks down to her feet like she's done something wrong. "Come here, Sweetheart," pulling her to sit on my knee. I lift her face to look at my face, "it's okay to not be fully alright, can you tell me what's going on up here?" tapping the side of her head. "Honestly, I think it's just my anxiety. Nothing that you've done. My brain just has a lot in it and it won't shut up. Plus, I'm mad at myself because I know better than to be rude. Not only was I rude but I did it in front of him." She nods over to Luther.

I can't help but smile at her. "Sweets, it's okay. I'm not mad, and I think I can speak for Luther, too, when I say you feeling safe enough to have an outburst is a good thing. Now tell me, what can I do to help you out of the weird headspace you're in?"

She taps her chin like she's actually thinking, "Um you could...OOOO, you could not spank me and have me take a shot of rum...you know rum over bum...yup, that sounds like a much better idea." She says it with such enthusiasm that neither I nor Luther can hold back our chuckles.

"Yeah, not gonna happen, Sweets. First, you don't mix liquors well at all, so that would put you in an inebriated state where we would be calling it a night. Second, using inebriation as a punishment or even as a relaxer is not safe. Is it?" Rose shakes her head, "Words please." She gives a quiet sigh, "No, Sir, and before you say it, I know. We don't repeat unhealthy coping mechanisms."

BREATHE

I smile, "Good girl, now is there anything I can actually do to help you feel better?" She doesn't take long to answer, "I don't think there is, right now, truthfully. Can we just get to it, Mr. Twitchyhand? I mean, Sir." Well, she's sassing so that's a good sign. "Alright, Sweetheart. What's your safeword?" I ask. "Pothos, Sir." There's a slight wobble to her voice but that's to be expected. I help her stand and lay over my knee with her chest to the couch. "And what's the club's safeword?" I ask. "Red, Sir." She responds, this time with a breathy voice. "Good girl."

I rub her back and look up at Luther. Holding my hand out, he passes over the basket to me with a nod. Sliding my hand down, I grab the bottom of her skirt and slide it slowly up over her beautiful round ass. I can't help but give her a light smack right over the pink hand marks that are still there from earlier, causing her to let out a little hiss. Satisfied that she's still with me, I go to slide her thong down her legs and she automatically lifts her hips for me like the good girl she is.

I can feel how turned on she is just by the dampness of her panties. I quickly put them in my breast pocket so I don't get distracted. Sliding my hand between her thighs I spread her legs wider, exposing her to me fully. *Fuck, she's so damn wet.* Sliding my finger through her wetness, I work my way up to the pretty little crystal shining in her back hole and start to twist it. Rose lets out a low moan as I slowly work the plug out. I set it in the small bowl provided in the basket and take out the lube and larger plug. I spread the lube on the plug first and then move over to her pretty puckered hole. It constricts with my movements, so I slide two fingers into her causing her to let out a gasping moan.

I continue to rub in and out of her while also scissoring my fingers to help open her further. I'm taking her from a small plug to a large one and I don't want to hurt her. It also doesn't hurt that even this is bringing her closer to the edge. When she starts panting I pull my fingers out of her and wipe my hands with a wet wipe. Taking the plug from my other hand, I move it to her hole and start easing it in.

She starts to wiggle in my lap, trying to rub herself on me, causing my erection to rub against my zipper with each little move. I look over at Luther and his eyes are pinned to what I'm doing. Clearing my throat, I ask, "Luther, you mind helping me out? Seems like someone is having trouble holding still."

His eyes snap up to mine and then back down to Rose, his voice sounds more like a growl when he asks her, "Are you okay with that Darlin'?" His voice seems to set something off in her because she moans out her yes more than says it. With a swift nod, Luther stands and walks over. Kneeling next to her on the couch he looks at me for directions.

I've seen him play before and this man may like to be called Daddy and loves to please, but is definitely one of the most dominant men I know. To see him kneeling and looking to me for direction is heady. "Pin her hips and spread her for me." With a smirk he nods and does what I've asked.

Going back to my task, I work the plug the rest of the way in, enjoying the sounds of her sexy whimpers the whole time. When the plug is finally fully seated I look up to see Luther with his lip between his teeth and his face contorted in both a mix of pleasure and pain. It's then I notice her hand has fallen down to his leg and she has one hell of a grip on his thigh.

*Hmmm, I wonder what would happen if...*I let my intrusive thought win and double tap the end of the plug. She lets out a deep moan and squeezes Luther's leg even harder causing him to look up at me with devilishly dark eyes. *Shit, that's hot.* Smiling, I wipe my hands down again and grab the U shaped combo g-spot and clitoral stimulator. "Now for your little something extra." It doesn't take me long to slide the toy into position. I can feel her trying to wiggle but with Luther's grip she isn't going anywhere.

"Alright Sweetheart, Luther is going to let go of your cheeks but still keep you pinned down, are you ready?" She nods but that simply will not do, "Words, Sweetheart," I remind her while I reach over and grab both remotes. "Yes, Sir. I'm ready." At that, I press both on buttons at the same time causing her to immediately jolt. "Shit, Sir, that's not fair!" Both Luther and I chuckle but it's Luther who responds to her, "No one ever said a Dom had to play fair."

CHAPTER 12

LUTHER

Oh, this bastard is sadistic, I love it. I slide my hands from Rose's squishable ass cheeks that make my mouth water to her hips. I watch as Harrison turns on the toys he's just put in her and feel her jolt. "Shit, Sir, that's not fair!" she whines. Neither of us can hold back our chuckles, this girl is fucking adorable. "No one ever said a Dom had to play fair."

Harrison growls as he sets the remotes down, "Now Sweetheart, count for me." I can feel my dick leaking as the first slap lands and I watch as her ass ripples from the impact. "One," Rose gasps out. I turn to look at her face just as the second slap lands. The mixture of both pain and pleasure I see there is overwhelming. "Two," If I feel this way just by watching, I know she must be on a whole other level.

Her grip on my thigh is so tight I know I'll have a bruise there tomorrow, but that just makes me even happier. I want this girl to leave her marks on me, to claim me as her own. She's doing so well. "Three." I bend down to her ear so only she can hear me, "You're doing so well Darlin', taking your punishment like such a good girl."

I feel her moan more than I hear it, watching as a chill runs down her spine. Catching Harrison's movement as he rears back again, I look at his face. I can tell he is fighting to stay in control. There is a hunger in his eyes that makes me weep in my jeans even more.

I've done scenes with guys before, and consider myself pretty sexually fluid. *What is it about Harrison that has my mouth salivating? Maybe it's how he handles Rose, or maybe it's the fact that I want to see how he falls apart too. Topping them both could be fun. I couldn't ever see myself being in a relationship with another man, but if he wanted to explore that hunger I see in him...I wouldn't say no.*

He brings his hand down, striking the junction where Rose's ass and thighs meet, the perfect location to thrust both toys deeper into her at the same time. Her gasping out, "Four," is just as much from the pain as it is from the pleasure I know just shot through her. Bringing his hand down one final time, he audibly strikes in the same spot as the last, I have to quickly tighten my hold as Rose tries to shoot herself up. "FIVEEEE," she damn near screams, her body trembling as waves of pleasure run through her. She's panting and I can tell she's close to the edge.

Rubbing my hand up her back to soothe her, I can't help but point it out to Harrison, "It seems like this little Darlin' is riding the edge." Leaning down I whisper in her ear, "Remember Darlin', you aren't allowed to cum unless you have permission." Picking up one of the remotes, he turns one of the toys off. I know it doesn't control both though because I can still feel the powerful vibration through her skin.

With a dark growl and even darker smile, Harrison finally responds to my statement. "You're absolutely right Luther, she is riding the edge. And the edge is where she will stay until she earns her orgasm." Helping her sit up in his lap, he continues. "Color, Sweetheart?"

She wiggles in his lap a bit before giving her answer. "Green, Sir." Her panting comes off with a bit of a purr. His smile widens, "Good girl. Now, you are going to sit between me and Luther and we are all going to finish our drinks. You are going to sit nicely while we do this, no wriggling about. When we are finished and only then will we move to the play area of the club. Be the good obedient girl that I know you can be for us, and I guarantee you will get the orgasm your body craves." His words have my dick jumping in my pants with need and anticipation. Fuck, these two are going to kill me tonight.

ROSE

It's official, I'm gonna explode. How am I supposed to sit here, and be still? The vibrations from the toy in my ass are still going strong, while the other toy is still in my pussy. *I was so close!* I should have known Harrison's 'light' punishment just meant light on the number of spankings not the actual actual punishment itself. This is just pure torture!

Harrison adjusts me to settle on the couch between him and Luther and I can feel the stickiness of my thighs. As soon as my tender ass connects with the couch, a stinging zap shoots through me causing me to moan. There's something both arousing and grounding about feeling the burn on your skin after a spanking. Right now I couldn't be more grateful for that. Sitting between these two men is dizzying. On my right, I have Harrison, the man I know can bring me over the cliff over and over again, for hours at a time. Then there's the man on my left. I may not know him well, but there is something about him that draws me in. Something about him tells me, when he brings me pleasure, I will never be the same.

CHAPTER 13

ROSE

I don't know how much longer I can hold out. It's been almost ten minutes and my body is screaming for release. Any time I move, the toys do too, driving me just that much crazier. I finished my drink almost immediately, but of course a glass of water showed up just as I was taking my last sip. Luther had thanked the waitress before she walked away while Harrison whispered in my ear, "Drink up, Sweetheart, we can't have you dehydrated now can we?"

Not willing to jeopardize my chances of being allowed to cum, I immediately picked it up and started drinking. I'm already three quarters of the way through, but the guys are still just sipping on their drinks. *Bastards, the both of them. I swear they are going slow on purpose.* Chugging the last bit of my water down, I lean forward to set my glass down and the toys shift again. This time hitting even deeper. My overstimulated body going on high alert ripping a guttural moan out of me. Both of their eyes fly to me as I try to shift myself back to a position that not flying over the edge into an orgasm is possible.

They must have had some form of communication because as I settle back again they are both finishing their drinks. "I think it's time we head to the play area," Harrison states before looking over my head. "Luther, you never answered earlier, care to join us?" The smile he shoots my way is devilish. "It would be a pleasure."

Standing, Harrison grabs my hand and we follow Luther through the lounge, towards the heavy black doors that lead into the club. As soon as Luther opens the door, the air of debauchery and lust fill my senses. The further we travel through the club the thicker it becomes, the beat and bass of the music throbbing and pulsing in time with both my heart and my clit. I can taste the sin on my tongue, and I love it.

I didn't realize just how much I missed this, the environment, the atmosphere, the pure carnal need. Add in the fact that with every step I take, the plug that is still vibrating deep inside me shifts, adding even more longing within me. I don't notice that I have been out of focus until Luther starts leading us down a hallway I've never been down.

Leaning over I squeeze Harrison's hand and ask, "Umm, Sir, where are we going? I didn't even know this area was back here." Grinning he fills me, "Apparently, we are getting the behind the scenes experience tonight." *Well that was cryptic.* Knowing Harrison's got me, though, I take a deep breath and continue following.

Luther stops at a small door towards the end of the hallway and pulls out a key card. Swiping it over a panel that is next to the door, I watch the light turn green. Luther opens the door and waves us in. The music in here is the same as it is in the belly of the club, just turned down enough to hear each other speak. A huge sofa is in the center of the room facing a blacked out glass panel. The cushions are so wide, the sofa could easily be considered a bed.

Leading me around to the front of the couch, Harrison has me sit right in the center while he kneels down in front of me. I can see that Luther is on the other side of the room and I turn to see what he's doing, but Harrison stops me, grabbing my chin and bringing my face to focus on him. I can't help but squirm, between the intense vibrations and his stare. "Sir, I thought we were going to the voyeur lounge?" I ask in a breathy voice. *Damn even I can hear the need in my voice.*

Harrison gives me a sneaky smile, "Luther, would you like to explain to Rose where we are?" Winking at me, Harrison uses his grip on my chin to turn my face towards Luther. He's standing next to another panel next to the glass, "Well, you see Darlin', there are some perks to being one of the owners of the club. This is a private viewing room that faces out to the voyeur play area," he presses something on the panel and the glass goes clear.

"Think of it as a private gallery. The glass is one way, looking like a giant mirror to anyone on the outside." That spurs a memory of signing my original membership contract. "This is what the contract meant by 'both seen and unseen monitoring'?" I blurt. "Yes, Darlin', consent in all things is key. Even when you say you want to be seen, you get to know how it will happen. Plus, anyone that steps into this club is subject to being watched in some form or fashion; even in the private play rooms. Safety is everything. Both of the private

BREATHE

viewing rooms we have set up, however, are only set up to watch the voyeur area."

Wanting some further clarification on why we are in this room instead of the main lounge, I ask, "So did you bring us here because it's private?" Nodding he continues, "I brought y'all here because of two reasons; the first is because it is secure and private, here you can be ravished properly without any possible interruptions. The second is so you can see things from a different point of view. Darlin', you have been tense since you walked through the front door tonight, I wanted you to be in a space where you can relax."

I can feel my eyes start to water. *He noticed, I've known this man for almost no time at all in the grand scheme of things and he freaking noticed!* "Thank you Luther," I go to adjust my positioning and the plug shifts inside me again. "MMMMM," I moan. "It means alot to me that you noticed." Shifting again I lean my head back as the sensations become overwhelming. I can't hold back any longer.

"AHHH, please, Sir, MMM, I can't!" Harrison makes a shushing noise towards me as he pulls the small remote out of his pocket, and taps it against his thigh. "Okay Sweetheart, you`ve been such a good girl," the vibrations in my ass get even stronger. Pulling out the second remote, I know what I'm in for. "Cum for me, Sweetheart." Harrison taps the button and I immediately feel like an electric shock has hit my body. *Is this thing on max or something?* My head flies back as the feeling intensifies.

"Yes, Fuckkkk, Sir."

"That's it, Sweetheart."

"I'm so close!" I somehow manage to pant out. Suddenly,

he leans up and latches his teeth down on my nipple. That's it, that's all I needed, I detonate. "SIIIRRRR" I scream, but he doesn't let up, not yet. My first orgasm starts to roll into another one and I swear the vibrations get more intense. I'm not sure if the scream that comes out of me is understandable or not but as a second more intense orgasm hits me I lose track of everything around me.

The vibrations shut off and Harrison works the toy out of my pussy, rubbing lightly to bring me down slowly. "That's my girl. You did so well, Sweetheart." I can't find my words so I just nod. "That was fucking beautiful, Darlin'." I roll my head and see Luther sitting on the far corner of the couch.

I give him what I hope is a seductive smile as I move to sit up. My movements cause Harrison to have to move too. Flopping down on the other side of me, Harrison is beaming with a self satisfied smirk. I know he sees me struggling just a bit though as soon as he comments, "Careful, Sweetheart, that endorphin rush was intense."

He goes to rise from the couch with that but Luther waves him back and stands instead. I can see the evidence of his arousal straining the front of his pants. *I want to taste him so bad.* I'm so focused on trying to see what Luther's doing, I don't see Harrison sliding up next to me.

Pulling me into his side, he whispers in my ear, "He's delicious isn't he?" *WHAT DID HE JUST SAY!?!?* My focus flies off of Luther and straight to Harrison, I swear I almost give myself whiplash. I lean in and whisper, "I didn't think you liked guys like that! When did this happen?"

He raises his eyebrows at me giving me the 'you want to try again' look causing me to backpedal. "Sorry Sir, you

BREATHE

caught me off guard." No sooner than those words leave my mouth do I have a blanket laid over me. *I swear these men are performing some kind of witchy juju. I can't focus on any one thing, damnit!* Harrison nods for me to adjust my focus just in time for Luther to hold out another glass of water to me. Thanking him, I take a sip and realize the drink might look like water, but is sweet.

I hear Luther chuckle when I look down at the glass like he handed me some ancient relic, and I'm supposed to discover all of its secrets. "It's just electrolytes, Darlin', that was a really intense punishment and we need to make sure you stay hydrated." I smile up at Luther, "Come sit with us?" I ask as I pat the seat next to me.

The smile he gives me is marvelous as he sits down "Thanks, Darlin'." I adjust and throw my legs over Harrison's and slightly lean back into Luther to test the waters. "So you said that they can't see in here right?" I ask looking up at Luther. "That's right, Darlin', you have a private room with a view tonight." He chuckles at his own joke, and I switch my attention to the scene unfolding in front of me.

The two men on the main stage are physically polar opposites. One is lean and built like a runner, while the other is muscular and reminds me a bit of a pro wrestler. The leaner man is the one leading the scene, while the larger of the two is the picture of submission. My excitement has peaked, I love watching others give in to their desires, even more when the typical roles are reversed.

I whisper under my breath "They're just so beautiful together," not expecting either one of the guys to hear me so I'm surprised when I hear them both murmur their agreements. The dominant stands behind his submissive giving off an air of confidence that is palpable even from here. Kneeling before his Dom completely naked, the muscular guy's cock is hard as steel. The leaner one stands before him with his slacks still on and reaches down, grabbing the one on his knees' hair. He pulls his head back and says something to him that I'm not able to hear, but it must have been something wicked, because even from my position I can see a shiver run down the other man's body. *Oh, this is gonna be good.*

The show is both beautiful and erotic. The way the dom truly leads his submissive to ecstasy is like a dance, and the trust they show each other is fluid as water. I feel the couch shift around me and for a moment I think I'm the one who's moved, until it happens again. It's then I notice that Luther keeps adjusting his leg, he's obviously aroused and trying to get more comfortable. *I wonder....*

"Mr. Breedlove, are you okay or would you prefer it if I moved?" My question brings both Luther and Harrison's attention to me. "What was that, Sweetheart?" Harrison asks, *hmmmm this could be fun,* "Well, Mr. Breedlove here seems to be uncomfortable, so I was simply offering to move, Sir." I try to make my voice innocent like I'm just being helpful.

"No Darlin', I don't want you to move. I quite like the feel of your body against mine." *Mmmm his voice is like velvet against my skin.* I don't stop my body's need to lean in to his further. "I can't say I mind the feeling of yours against mine either, Mr. Breedlove." He moves to rub his hand against me but stops part way there, "May I touch her?" *Excuse the hell out of you mister! Why are you asking him!*

My thoughts must be written all across my face because

Harrison roars with laughter. "I'm perfectly okay with that, but I think you might want to ask Rose. She looks like she wants to bite both of our heads off." Luther brings his eyes down to mind and smirks, "May I touch you, Darlin'?" I cross my arms over my chest with a hmph, "Oh, now I get to choose?" I know I sound like a petulant child but hell, it's my damn body.

"Darlin', the choice is always yours, but," Luther points at my bracelet, "that pretty piece of jewelry there says no matter what, I have to ask your Sir, first." *Well shit I forgot about the charm on my wrist.* "Oh, I forgot about that," I uncross my arms and lower my eyes. "I'm sorry, Mr. Breedlove, of course you can touch me." Luther slides his hand up and down one arm, while using his free hand to lift my chin so I'm looking back in his deep chocolate eyes. "Don't hide from us Darlin', no one here will do you any harm."

Come on Rose, get it together girl. "It's nothing like that Mr. Bre–," He places his thumb at my mouth causing my breath to catch. "No more Mr. Breedlove. It's Luther, Darlin', at least for now." There's a note of promise in his voice that sends a shiver down my spine. "Luther," his name comes out almost as a sigh. "It's not that I think y'all will hurt me. If I'm being honest..." *Just spit it out, Rose.*

"What is it then, Sweetheart?" Harrison encourages from my other side. He's rubbing my feet and ankles now and damn does it feel good. Steeling myself I push forward, "If I'm being honest, I feel stupid for forgetting." Turning to Harrison, I continue, "I'm sorry for forgetting you're the one fully in control tonight, Sir. I let myself get completely lost in the feeling of the moment."

Harrison moves his hands even higher, now rubbing my inner thigh. "That's okay, Sweetheart, that's what you're supposed to do." Luther's hand that had been on my chin starts rubbing over my collar bone, while his other hand begins rubbing my torso. I gasp at the feeling, I know Harrison is okay with my body shape, but not everyone enjoys the feel of a bigger girl. It took me a long time to love the body I have, and I rarely become self conscious of others opinions.

There's something about Luther though, I want him to want me as I am. My trepidation must be written on my face, because Harrison quickly steps in to ease my fears. "Her body feels amazing, doesn't it, Luther?"

Luther lets out a deep growl that runs down all the way to my pulsing core. "Feels like absolute perfection. I'm salivating at just the thought of tasting her soft skin, my hands are aching to run themselves over every inch of her. I don't think I have ever been this hard at just the thought of touching someone." The pressure of both their touches increases as he speaks. My body is so hot I feel like I'm laying on a bed of coals.

"How does that sound to you, Sweetheart? Do you want Luther to touch your body? To taste your skin? To help bring you over the edge?" I groan at the thought, I can feel my core dripping at the picture they have painted. "Yes, Sir. I think I would really like that." The words are barely out of my mouth, when Luther flicks his tongue over my ear. *UGHHHH that feels so good.* I feel Harrsion shift again moving closer to us and causing my legs to open further. He slides his hands even higher, now right at the point where my thighs meet my pussy.

Moaning, I ask the question I had originally wanted to ask before things escalated. "Luther?" He nips my ear, "Yes, Darlin'?" *Fuck his voice is sexy,* "You were turned on by the show..." "Mmmm, yes, it did drive my arousal higher, Darlin'." *I need to know,* "Have you ever played with another man?" I feel Harrison's ministrations stutter for a moment so I bring my gaze down to his while I wait for Luther's answer.

"Yes, Darlin', I have. If you're asking what my sexuality is, I'll tell you this, I don't put myself in any single box. I play with whomever pleases my senses." I nod slightly at his response, I'm still holding Harrison's gaze and see the burst of flame there. "Does that bother you, Darlin'?" Shaking my head slightly, I give him my truth. "No, honestly, it's a turn on. I love seeing two men in the throws of passion together. There's something primal and almost violent about it."

I watch Harrison lift my dress at the same time I feel Luther bend and run his tongue up my neck. "Delicious." "Is that something you want to see, Sweetheart?" I moan my agreement, unable to form the words with the onslaught of sensation they are giving me. Harrison maneuvers me off his lap, pulling me to sit up so he can take off my dress and bra.

The small break is welcome. There's one more thing I need to ask. "What about you Harrison? Have you ever played with another man?" I can see the wheels turning in his mind as he lays me out on the end of the chaise. "I have been in scenes where other men were involved, but never where they or I touched each other. I can't say I wouldn't participate though. It's just never happened that way."

I'm spread out for these two beautiful men, fully naked and aching with the need for them to touch me. Harrison bends my legs and settles between them, while Luther kneels on the floor near my head. "Luther, I'm starving and I see you are too. Enjoy her body, while I devour this sweet pussy, will ya?" The grin that crosses Luther's face is wicked. "It would be my pleasure."

My legs are pushed back as Harrison settles in further between them. The feel of his breath on my molten core causes me to whimper in anticipation, but he doesn't make me wait long. The first slow swipe of his tongue has my back bowing off the couch with a gasp. *Ffffuuuccckkk.*

Luther lets out a low groan at my response and slides his hand up my torso to my right breast, kneading my nipple with a firm pressure that mixes with the sensations Harrison's causing. His other hand moves into my hair taking it in a tight grasp near the scalp. Pulling just a bit, he causes my head to lean back and he licks up from my collar bone to my ear, taking my lobe into his mouth. I gasp as Harrison spears me with his tongue at the same time Luther both bites down on my earlobe and pinches my nipple.

"Oh shit, yesssss," I hiss. Luther releases my lobe but stays near my ear. Just the sound of his breathing is erotic to me. I try to turn to him, hungry for his lips on mine, but he tightens his grip, halting my movements and causing me to whimper. "Shhhh Darlin', it's okay, but I won't be kissing your lips tonight. When I kiss your lips for the first time, it will be me claiming them as my own. Not me being under another man's power." He says it so low I know it was only meant for me to hear, like it's our little secret.

He nips my ear again, before slowly running his tongue down my body down to my left breast. I'm vibrating under their touch, my climax climbing closer to the cliff's edge. Harrison switches the hold he has on my thigh and starts suckling directly on my clit in slow deep pulls. I can't see him but the sounds coming from him tells me he's enjoying this just as much as I am.

Luther runs his tongue around my erect nipple before taking it into his mouth fully. I feel Harrison thrust two fingers into me at the same time and I can't hold back my scream. *It's too much, they are going to kill me.* Harrison curls the fingers inside of me in a come hither motion, while keeping the same tempo on my clit and I feel my legs start to shake. Harrison moves his other hand from my thigh while Luther peppers kisses back up to my ear. Pulling my head back by my hair once more, he winds his hand around my throat. Bringing his mouth back to my ear he whispers, "You look so beautiful laid out at our mercy."

The intense vibrations start in my ass again causing me to moan loudly. I'm panting as he continues, "Now be a good girl, and show me just how spectacular you look when you cum," he leans back, "NOW!" With that he leans back into my neck and bites down just as Harrison clamps down hard on my clit and I detonate screaming both of their names. I'm not sure how long I'm floating in absolute heaven, but as I come down I hear them both praising me between kisses on my skin.

"So beautiful, Darlin'."

"Such a good girl for us, Sweetheart,"

"A man could die happy just at the sight of you climaxing, Darlin',"

"That's it, Sweetheart, come back to us."

When I'm finally back in my own body, I move to sit up. "Y'all's turn," but they both stop me from touching them. "No, Sweetheart, this was about you." *Wait what?* "Well shit!" Luther smoothes back my hair before Harrison helps me sit up. I go to pull Harrison down beside me but he stops me. "I've gotta go grab stuff to clean you up, Sweetheart. Why don't you and Luther snuggle up and I'll be right back." He nods at Luther and turns to move towards the door.

"Harrison there is a sink and a towel warmer hidden in that cabinet there, no need to leave." I snuggle into Luther's side as Harrison preps the cloths and comes over. "You did so well for us, Sweetheart," he says as he works to clean my body, "why don't I finish up here and then we can snuggle for a bit." Nodding I relax into them, I'm not sure how long it's been when I feel someone shaking me lightly. *What the hell, who is waking me up?*

"Hey Darlin', time to wake up. You have to get home." I mumble something I'm pretty sure was close to *I don't want to wake up*, but I can't be sure. "She's really out of it," I hear Luther say to Harrison. "Yeah she is, I'm going to stay with her tonight to watch for drop. Don't worry, I'll take care of her." Harrison is always so sweet to me. Feeling a little more awake, I grumble "The her in question is right here and I'll be fine," *There that will show them.*

"That might be the case, but it's not up for discussion, Sweetheart. I'm staying with you tonight and that's final." I can't help the pout that takes over my face and look up to

Luther. I'm not sure why, but I want to know what he thinks. "Don't look at me like that, Darlin'. I agree with Harrison. You shouldn't be alone tonight." *Drat they are working together on this too.*

"Harrison, you have my number, I would appreciate it if you would text me tomorrow and let me know how she's doing." *GRRRR* "AGAIN, the she in question is right here!" I huff at them. Tipping my hair back Luther continues, "Well, oh impatient one, if you wouldn't have interrupted I would have already gotten to this, but I would also really like it if you would call or text me tomorrow, as well. I know y'all's phones are locked up so you'll have to get my number from Harrison, but I really hope to hear from you." My heart flutters and I nod, "I can do that." His smile is brilliant, "Good girl."

It's not long after that I'm finishing getting dressed with the help of Harrison. Luther walks over with my heels in one hand, but has a pair of sandals in the other. "These will be more comfortable for you to walk out in." Bending down he sets them in front of the correct feet and holds my hand as I step in.

"Are you ready, Sweetheart?" I keep hold of Luther's hand as I turn to look at Harrison. "Yes, Sir." Grabbing my other hand Harrison leads us to the front. "Thank you for sharing tonight, Harrison, you have given me a gift I will never forget." Turning me to him fully, Luther rubs his thumb across my cheek, "And thank you, Darlin', you didn't have to trust me tonight but you did. That is a gift and a blessing I will never take for granted. I look forward to hearing from you." Placing a kiss on my opposite cheek, he starts to back away, but I stop him. "Thank you, Luther. I'll talk to you tomorrow, good night." Smiling he simply says "Good night, Darlin', before turning and walking away.

Grabbing my hand, Harrison leads me out of the club. "Let's get you home, Sweetheart. You have had one eventful night." The whole way home the only thing I can think about are molten chocolate eyes and the promise of things to come.

CHAPTER 14

ROSE

Waking up Sunday morning, I'm not sure which feeling is stronger. The excitement that my best friend is coming home today, or the fear that she's not going to want me as her person anymore. Rolling over I grab my phone to check the time... *Uggghhh it's only 8!* Grumbling under my breath, I open my messaging app that's lit with 2 new conversation alerts. I don't even try to stop the smile that takes over my face when I see I have messages from both Harrison and Luther. Flopping back down, I open my message thread with Harrison first:

HARRISON

Mornin' BooBear! You better have gotten a good night's sleep, even though this teddy bear wasn't there to snuggle you!

I'll be over around 9 to help you get everything together for today! I'm bringing breakfast, so get your ass up!

Text me! Love you!

CRAAAAPP! Now I don't have a choice but to get up. Asshole's always on time.

Groaning, I reply,

ME

> Morning... you aren't a teddy bear, you're a pain in my ass. 9 a.m. is too damn early. You better be coming with a bomb ass breakfast and caffeine if you want me to let you in the door.

> Also...I hope you know I hate you with all my left tittie.

He replies before I can close out the thread.

HARRISON

> You know you love me! I'm also not stupid enough to show up first thing in the morning and NOT bring you the gogo juice.

> Now! GET UP! I'll see you in an hour!

ME

> FINE 😒!! I'll see you then!

Exiting our thread, I roll over to my side and open my messages from Luther.

LUTHER

> Good Morning Darlin'. I hope you slept beautifully.

Gahhh this man is so sweet!

> ME
> Good Morning! I slept okay, I guess. I will say waking up to a text message from you is quite nice.

Is that weird? God I hope he doesn't think I'm some clingy, needy, female. I mean I am, but I don't want him thinking that... We texted on and off all day yesterday after I texted him to check in. He had the butterflies in my stomach going the whole time.

> LUTHER
> You were the first thought I had this morning. Why was your sleep just 'okay you guess'? Everything alright?

BE STILL MY HEART!!!! THIS MAN!!! Do men like this actually exist? Sighing, I decide if he really wants to know and really wants to know me, I'll give him the truth.

> ME
> I think it might have been the nerves I'm feeling about today. Kat is coming home and I'm scared she might still be mad at me or even hate me now.

He must still have our conversation open because he is replying almost immediately.

> LUTHER
> Who's Kat and why would she be mad at you?

ME

She's my best friend who also happens to be my roommate. She's been my person forever.

She also is the girl who was attacked that night at Peaks. After that night she slipped into a really severe depression and had to check into a therapy hospital.

LUTHER

So why would she be mad at you for that? You didn't attack her or cause her to be hospitalized.

ME

Well that's partially true. I didn't attack her, you're right. But...

LUTHER

But what Darlin'?

ME

Well...I'm the one who called her aunt and told her that she wasn't okay. Her aunt is the one who had her admitted. So, it kinda is my fault she got hospitalized.

LUTHER

Oh sweet girl, it's not your fault. Sounds like you were worried about her and did all you could do to help her. The only person who is at fault is the ass who attacked her.

ME

We've talked about it since and she says we are fine and she understands. I still worry she won't want anything to do with me anymore though.

> **LUTHER**
> I think it'll be okay Darlin'.

> **ME**
> I hope you're right.

Looking up at the time I see it's already almost 8:30. *Shit, I need to hurry up and shower.*

> **ME**
> I just realized what time it is. Harrison will be here in like 30 minutes to help me fix up the apartment and I still need to get up and shower.

> **LUTHER**
> Go shower Darlin' and text me later.

> **ME**
> You know it 😉

Dragging myself out of bed I head to the kitchen to grab a coffee. Do I know Harrison's bringing me some? Yes. Do I care? No. Caffeine is life. As soon as the coffee maker starts up, my bladder aggressively lets me know I have to pee. Rushing to the bathroom, I swear my body sings with joy as soon as I sit down. I finish up and turn on the shower. No reason to take a cold shower.

Heading back to the kitchen, I grab my coffee from the maker and doctor it up how I like it. *Alright, shower time.* Luckily, I don't need to wash my hair or anything this morning. So it doesn't take long for me to drink my coffee and wash up in the shower. Drying off I decide today is an official comfy day, no makeup and no real effort required. Brushing my hair and tossing it up in a ponytail before I head back to the room solidifies my decision.

I grab my water off my side table before heading to my dresser to grab my clothes and take my meds. Popping my meds in my mouth, the stupid pill goes down sideways getting caught in my throat. *OUCH!* I finally get it down after chugging what's left of my water but I can only hope that's not an omen for what the day will bring.

I grab my stretchy black leggings out of the bottom drawer and a cute but comfy green tank top from the middle. When I go to grab my bra out of my top drawer the blasted drawer is stuck. Fuck it, Harrison can fix it when he gets here. I've just finished putting my clothes on when Harrison does his signature knock on the front door. Checking the peephole to make sure it's him before I open the door, I see him standing in our hallway with his hands full.

I open the door with the chain lock still on and smile at him. "What's the password?" He chuckles and gives me a look that tells me he knows I'm being a shit on purpose. "Well, I do believe the password is, I have both coffee and an energy drink for you, along with your favorite omelet. Closely followed by the backup password of let me in or you have to do all the cleaning and organizing by yourself."

Damn he knows my weaknesses all too well. "Access Granted!" Closing the door for just a second I remove the chain lock and open the door fully so he can walk in. "You're a little shit, you know that?" he shoots at me as he walks by. "Excuse me, but aren't you the one who gave me shit for not being careful enough? I was just being thorough and making sure you weren't body snatched or somethin!" Shooting him a wink I bounce over to the smorgasbord he's set on the counter.

The coffee smells divine and I can't wait to dive in. Harrison clears his throat, making me move my attention to him. "What??" I ask with a whine. As soon as our eyes connect, he lifts his brow. Sighing, I give him what he obviously wants. "Thank you Harrison for making sure I don't starve or go to jail for murder this morning." He gives me a sharp nod, "You're welcome, now eat up so we can get busy."

Once we are well fed and fully caffeinated we get started on getting the apartment together. Harrison works on the bathroom and kitchen since he knows those are the rooms I loathe working on the most. While I work on the bedroom and living room. I strip Kat's bed and throw her sheets in the washer before going back to make mine.

I look at my side table and figure I better grab all of my random empty cups and take them in the kitchen before Harrison starts the dishes. I promise you, if I brought out a bunch of dirty cups right as he's finishing, he would whoop my ass. Between my side table and dresser I take out five glasses, three coffee cups, and two bowls.

Harrison looks at me with exacerbation as I walk towards the kitchen, "Rose, is it really so hard to bring your dirty dishes to the sink after you use them?" I just giggle at him. If there are two things that I struggle with when it comes to my ADHD, it's actually putting my dishes in the sink and object permanence. "Half the time I set them down and then forget they are there. At least there aren't doom piles all around the apartment! Small wins Harrison, take them!" I hear him groan as I walk back into the room.

An hour later, I've managed to fold and put up all the laundry, dust, actually clean up my side table, and I'm finally at the point where I just need to vacuum. Grabbing the small vacuum out of the closet, I do a good once over on the floor and then hop up onto Kat's bed. I wobble a bit, but catch myself on the wall. The thud my hand makes as it hits the wall though, sounds like I've crashed and burned...HARD.

"WHAT WAS THAT?" I hear from the other room. "Ummm, just me hittin' the wall! Nothing to worry about!" I yell back as I steady myself and get ready to start. Just as I go to turn on the little sucker that could, Harrison stands in the doorway, "Why the hell are you standing on Kat's bed?"

"Umm, isn't it obvious? I'm working on my suction skills, Duhhh!" *He really makes it too damn easy.* "Okay smartass..." Rolling my eyes, I give him his answer, "I'm just going to vacuum Kat's bed, nothing insane. The attachment's busted so I can't lay it flat anymore." Seemingly pleased with this answer he just shakes his head as he walks back out. It doesn't take me long to finish up in here, and I head out to grab Kat's sheets and move her comforter to the dryer.

I'm shocked at what I see when I walk out. This man in the 2 hours it's taken me to clean our room has done the kitchen, the bathroom, and has most of the living room picked up. "Holy shit, how in the hell did you manage to get all this done when I've only just finished our room?"

Chuckling he walks over and grabs both my cheeks and squishes them together, "I'm a wizard Rose, I just waved my wand and used '*focius cleanius*'." Kissing my forehead he turns away and goes back to what he was doing. *Butthead, there was no need to use my favorite movie to tease me.*

Between the two of us it doesn't take long for us to finish the rest of the living room and to make up Kat's bed after that.

Hearing my phone go off in the kitchen I run to grab it. The screen lights up and I see I have multiple missed notifications. Ignoring my social alerts, I move to open my messages. *Apparently, I've been a bit MIA today... Oops.*

> **KRYSTAL**
>
> Hey munch, I'm headed to go pick KitKat up now. I'll let you know when I get there.
>
> Just pulled into the facility! It's gonna take an hour or two to get everything squared up here then we will be on our way.

Shit she sent that last one over an hour ago!

> **ME**
>
> Hey Krys! Sorry, I was cleaning and didn't hear my phone! Yes, please let me know when yall leave! Love you!

Knowing she's busy, I move onto the other conversations.

> **BIRTH GIVER**
>
> Rose, we need to speak about the gym membership and meal prep subscription I gave you for your birthday. I just spoke with the owner and she said you never contacted her to activate the plan. Call me when you get the chance.

Yeah, I really can't deal with her today, So I just close out that conversation. The next one makes me smile.

> **LUTHER**
> Hi beautiful, I just wanted you to know I have been thinking about you all day. I know I told you to text me later, so I don't expect a response, but I hope you are having a fantastic day.

> **ME**
> I don't know about fantastic since we have been cleaning all morning, but it's not bad. I hope your day is going great though!

My phone vibrates with another incoming message,

> **KRYSTAL**
> That's okay munch, we've gotten all the paperwork signed already. Now we are just packing her stuff up in the car. We should be there in a little over an hour. Love you too!

An hour, in just an hour I'll find out if she truly forgives me, or if I've lost my best friend forever. My heart feels like it's going to beat out of my chest. So, I set my phone down and head to the couch. Tears are beginning to fill my eyes before I ever reach the living room. Harrison must notice because as soon as I flop down he's right there in front of me. "What's wrong, BooBear? Tell me what happened."

"I'm scared," I sniffle out, "What if she decided I'm not her person anymore? She said I betrayed her before. What if she actually still feels that way?"

Harrison squeezes me tight before pulling me back to look me straight in the eye. "BooBear, she told you she didn't actually feel that way when you went to see her. It was the confusion and trauma talking. I thought y'all worked that out in your joint shrinky-dink session." I can't help but giggle at the way he said that, and I'm positive that's why he did it. "I mean she did, but like did she mean it?"

"What do you mean?"

"Well, that day she told me 'I don't fully remember what I said that day to you. What I do remember is blaming you and yelling that I would never forgive you. For that, I am so sorry, I was in a haze and you were the easiest person to attack, you didn't do anything wrong.' but I can't help but worry that she changed her mind."

It's with those words the dam that has been holding back my tears, completely breaks. Harrison, being the amazing man that he is, just holds me as I cry on his shoulder. I finally start to pull myself together and pull back, his shirt is soaked on his shoulder. He doesn't seem to care, though, and just reaches up to wipe my eyes.

"Everything is going to be okay. I'll be right here with you okay?" I just nod and focus on my breathing to try and calm down. *UGHHHH My nose is all stuffy now!* Standing, I head back to the kitchen and blow my nose aggressively. "Dang girl! Are you trying to sound an alarm with that blow!"

"Oh, shove it!" *Dumbass.* Grabbing my phone I walk back to the couch. I curl into Harrison's side.

Unlocking it automatically opens to my messages with Krystal. Looking at the time, that message was sent thirty minutes ago. Clicking out of that thread, I click into my conversation with Luther to see a new message waiting for me.

> **LUTHER**
>
> What can I do to help make your day fantastic Darlin'?

> **ME**
>
> Just talking to you makes me smile. I'm currently laying on Harrison trying not to think...
>
> Kat is on her way.

> **LUTHER**
>
> It'll be okay Darlin'. Is Harrison gonna stay with you tonight?

> **ME**
>
> I know he's staying for awhile, but I don't know if he is staying the night.

> **LUTHER**
>
> Tell him I said he would be an idiot if he doesn't stay.

Giggling, I show Harrison the message from Luther. "HA! Tell him he can bite me. Also, I can't stay the night but I will be hanging out for a while." Looking up into his eyes I ask, "Why CAN'T you stay the night?" Poking my nose he responds, "I have a meeting at 5:30 in the morning, and I don't know if you have met either of y'all in the morning but...NO THANK YOU!" He finishes tickling my side. Both of us go back to our phones.

> **ME**
>
> Harrison told me to tell you he said bite me.

LUTHER
It would be my pleasure 🐻

ME
Oh would it now?

    Looking back up at Harrison I show him Luther's reply. I can feel the shiver that runs through his body as he reads. His eyes meet mine and I can see this confused lust that's within them. I give him a reassuring smile to let him know I don't see anything wrong with it.

"Have you ever...?"

"No, BooBear, I have...to be honest, until recently I really haven't felt the urge to. I've always been able to appreciate the male form, but lately it's been more..." my sweet Harrison looks so lost.

"You want to explore?" I can tell he is really thinking about his answer. Before he can come to a conclusion there's a knock at the door. Peeking at the time, I know...Kat's finally home.

CHAPTER 15

ROSE

*R*ushing to the door, I look out the peephole before I yank the door all the way open. At the same time, we say each other's names.

"Kat..."

"Rose..."

And with that, we fling ourselves into each other's arms. This hug feels like a patch being sewn onto a beloved coat you know you could never give up. I swear I can feel the fibers of who we are and we're stitching together the longer we hold each other.

Rarely, people come into your life that are part of your forever. Call it twin flames, call it soulmates, call it whatever you want. When you meet these people, you just know. You know that no matter what happens they will be by your side. They won't judge you, they won't leave, and if you fight you will always come back together.

We pull away from each other, tears running down both of our cheeks. "I'm so damn glad you're home." I cry. "Not as glad as I am, being home." We hug again, but it doesn't last long before we hear Krystal from behind Kat.

"Umm this is sweet and all, but these damn bags are heavy!" Laughing we move out of the way and let Krys in. Stepping up, Harrison pulls Kat in for a quick hug and asks Krys, "Is this everything?" Krystal gives a 'you're kidding, right' chortle before simply stating "Really?!?!?!?" Laughing, Harrison hugs her around the shoulders and leads her out the door to grab the rest of Kat's gear.

I'm smiling as I turn back to Kat. "They are both something else." I go to walk into the kitchen, but the hand she locks on my elbow stops me. "I've missed you, Rose. I have felt like the other half of me has been missing this entire time. I want you to know I meant every word I said that day at the hospital. I never meant any of the hateful things I spewed at you. You didn't betray me. I gave up on me and took it out on you. I hope you can forgive me." As she speaks more tears spill from her eyes. I grab her and hug her as tight as I can, "There's nothing to forgive. I'm just happy you don't hate me. I love you, girly. Always and Forever."

Just then Harrison steps through the door and lets out a loud gagging sound. Turning his head he raises his voice and yells out, "Krystal! They are doing the sappy crying shit again! I think I may need to leave with you!"

It's been a few hours since Kat got home and now we are ordering dinner while curled up in the living room. "Y'all know sushi doesn't really go with butterbeer and it doesn't count as a wizard meal right?" Harrison asks us with a look of pure exacerbation on his face.

"Umm, You know you're wrong, right?" I sass back at him.

"Oh, really? How's that?" Harrison asks, before I can reply Kat chimes in with, "Because, sweet Harrison, sushi is magic in your mouth." With his mouth hanging, I watch Harrison hit order on his delivery app.

Feeling sassy, I shoot back at him, "No arguments, big guy?" I can see the wheels turning in his head. "Nope, it's safer to just roll with it and feed y'all. Plus, with you two together, I'm fighting an uphill battle."

Satisfied, I take a sip of my drink, "Wow, these are strong Kat, at this rate we will be too hammered to watch the whole movie!" Rolling her eyes at me she says, "Look I've been locked up, this bitch really needed a drink! Plus, we've watched this series a million times." Laughing we settle in and hit play on the movie.

A few hours later, our food has been destroyed and we are all chunky and comfy. Kat is asleep on the couch and I'm struggling to keep my eyes open myself. Harrison turns off the TV as the credits start to roll, standing he declares it's bed time for us both and starts picking up the mess in the living room.

"I can do that," I say as he moves to take our empty glasses to the kitchen. "I know you can," he says, "but I'm going to do it while you go get ready for bed." I pout at him but he just points to the bathroom telling me with the move to not argue and just do it. "What time do you need to be at work in the morning?" Harrison asks as I head into the bathroom. "I don't, I took tomorrow off to spend with Kat and take her to meet with Jas."

I open the bathroom door to the most adorable sight. Harrison is carrying Kat into our joint bedroom to put her to bed. The little snores she's letting out tells me the butterbeer thoroughly did their job. I stand at the door and watch him tuck her in and smile at the fact he has already put water and some pain relief on her bedside table. Whispering, he asks, "Do you know where her phone is?"

"No, the service was paused since she couldn't have it. We will have to get it turned back on tomorrow." Walking back into the living room together, I see that he has already fully cleaned up our mess except for the throw blankets, so I walk over to fold them. He hasn't moved from the entrance and when I look at him, he has a strange look on his face. "What's up, Harrison?"

"I think I do..." *Uh what?*

"Do what?"

"I think I do want to explore. I mean I don't know that I could, one on one...but maybe if you were there...I don't know...maybe it's stupid..." I rush over to him and hug the crap out of him. "It isn't stupid, Harrison. I'm here for you in any way you need me to be."

"Thank you, BooBear."

"Always"

Harrison heads home, and I grab my phone before heading to bed. Laying there I open my messages, knowing I've been ignoring my phone for hours.

MATT

Yo! I called you but you didn't answer. Figured you are busy. Just wanted to check in and see how this afternoon went. Let me know and I'll see you on Tuesday!

ME

Sorry, I've been ignoring my phone. It went really well. We will talk more Tuesday! Night!

Moving on to the next message, I groan internally,

BIRTH GIVER

Rose, I do not appreciate being ignored! Call me back immediately!

ME

Sorry Mom. I've been really busy today. I'll try to call you tomorrow.

Gag me, I do not want to deal with this woman. Moving on...

LUTHER

I think it might...

Maybe I shouldn't have said that.

ME

No I'm glad you did 😊

Sorry I didn't respond earlier. I was ignoring my phone to be present. Harrison just left and now I'm getting ready to go to bed. Night!

Scrolling through my socials for a few minutes, I quickly

get bored. *I do believe it's 'audiobook and crash' time.* Putting on my sleep headphones and my comfort listen, *SICKO* by Amo Jones, I slowly start to drift away.

CHAPTER 16

ROSE

Waking up the next morning feels surreal. Hearing Kat breathing on the other side of the room brings me peace, and for a moment I just lay there and listen. I know I should get up, but peace is so rare in my life lately, I just want to enjoy it. It doesn't take long for my bladder to let me know that my bed is no longer the place to be. I sneak out of the room trying to be as quiet as possible. I would hate to wake Kat up by accident with it being her first morning home.

An hour and two cups of coffee later, Kat walks into the kitchen. "Yumm, bacon!" I lightly smack her hand away as she reaches for the slices currently draining on the plate next to me. "Those just came out of the pan, if you touch them now you will burn yourself."

"BUTTTTT ROOOSSEEE, IT SMELLS SOOOO GOOD!!!!!!" She whines. Giggling at her antics I point over to the bar. "Sit. I made your favorites."

"OOOO, You made your french toast?" I swear her excitement is infectious.

"Yes ma'am, I did! Stuffed with cream cheese and all. I only waited to do the bacon last, because I knew the smell would get you out of bed. So, go sit down and wait for your breakfast."

"Ma'am, yes, ma'am!" She takes two steps before stopping. Kat looks longingly at the coffee pot and then at me. Moving her eyes back to the coffee she barely gets out an "Ummm," before I chuckle and relieve her of the question. "Yes, Kat, make your coffee!"

We are sitting on the couch after breakfast catching up. It's nice having my best friend back, I don't feel so alone.

"So wait, let me see if I've got this right," Kat starts. "You hadn't been to the club at all until this past weekend because of me?" She looks like just the thought of me holding back because of what happened hurts her.

"I wouldn't say my fear was because of you," I soothe her. "It's more about what happened to you, that's what triggered my resistance. All my trust in the system kinda went out of the window." Sighing I grab her hand. "You are my person and seeing you broken, broke something in me. I was scared that it would happen again"

"But you went to F.O.U.R.S. this weekend?"

"Yeah."

"And Harrison black beaded you?"

"Yes."

"But while you were there you ran into the delicious man-sspreso that you met at the coffee shop?"

I full belly laugh at that. "Yes, his name is Luther."

"And he owns the club?"

"Partially, yes."

"And y'all played together?"

"Again, yes. Are you going to just keep recapping everything I've told you?" I fake scoff.

"Bitch, I'm so damn jealous! I haven't gotten laid in months!" Kat squeals, bouncing on her seat like crazy.

"Well, if we are being technical... Neither have I."

"Wait, wait, wait! You're telling me this man, Luther, played with you and Harrison, but you didn't fuck his brains out?"

"That's what I'm saying. No penises went into the Terminator." I say pointing at my crotch with both hands.

"OMG I can not believe you! Also, eww, you've got to stop calling your pussy that."

I give her a thoroughly offended look, "Why would I do that?!? Once they've had it, THEY'LL BE BACK"

We both break out into school girl giggles. *Damn, I've missed this.* Pulling myself back together, I try to figure out how I'm going to ask my next question.

"Just ask me, Rose. I can see you have a question." Taking a deep breath I go for it, "I know you said you're feeling better, but are you planning on rejoining F.O.U.R.S.? I know playing used to be your way to escape."

Kat lets out a deep sigh, "Truthfully, I wouldn't be opposed to it at some point. I don't think I'm at the point where I could see myself submitting to anyone right now though. Doesn't matter right now, anyways," she gives me a sad smile. "I'm officially jobless for now, so I couldn't afford to go if I wanted to."

"What the hell! What happened to your job?"

"Well, when you don't show up and call out constantly for weeks, employers don't particularly like that."

"But you've been giving me rent every month?"

"Savings, I have enough for the next four months until our lease is up. If I don't find anything by then, I'll probably have to move back home."

I will be damned if she is forced back to that hell hole. "We'll figure it out! I won't let you end up back there." And I won't, I'll cover rent for now until she can find something. "I'll ask Matt tomorrow if we have any openings." She gives me a small smile.

"Okay, Rose. Hey, can we go swimming? It's been crazy hot and they didn't have a pool at the hospital."

Letting her change the subject for now, I smile. "Yeah Kat, let's get ready. I do have to be back up by 4 though. I have therapy today."

Sitting outside of Jas's office, I'm smiling down at my phone. If this man gets any sweeter I just might get a cavity.

LUTHER
So did you and your bestie have a good day today?

ME
We did! We went down to the pool and soaked for a bit. Now I'm just waiting to go into therapy. How's your day going?

LUTHER
It's been a good day. Busy like any other Monday, but not crazy. I am running into a bit of a dilemma today tho…

ME

Oh, what's the problem? Anything I can help with?

LUTHER

There's this beautiful girl that I've been talking to and I would love to ask her on a date.

I'm not sure she would be interested though. What do you think...should I ask her?

ME

Oh, I didn't know you were talking to someone. Does she seem like she likes you?

LUTHER

I think so...

ME

Do you like her?

LUTHER

I really do.

ME

Then if it were me, I would ask her. You'll have to let me know what she says.

LUTHER

So what do you say Darlin'?

ME

What do I say?

LUTHER
Would you like to go on a date with me?

ME
Wait a minute!!! YOU WERE TALKING ABOUT ME THIS WHOLE TIME?!?!

LUTHER
Who did you think I was talking about Darlin'?

ME
😊 I swear I can't with you.

LUTHER
Are you rolling your eyes at me Darlin'?

ME
Gotta head into therapy! Talk to you later!

Giggling as I get out of the car, I head into the building for my appointment. I'm feeling light for the first time in a long time, I've forgotten how good it could feel. Today has been amazing.

CHAPTER 17

ROSE

I saunter into Jas's office with a pep in my step and a smile on my face. Flopping down on her couch with a giggle, I give her a smile as I say, "What up, Doc?"

"Well, hello Rose. Looks like someone is in a good mood today. Do tell me what has you smiling like this."

I stop to really think about what has me in such a good mood. Today has been such a day of smiles, I'm not sure I could pinpoint just one. "Really, it's just been an amazing day."

Jas makes that humming sound in the back of her throat that people make when they are curious about something. "Tell me then, what has made today so amazing?"

So I do. Starting from last night all the way through till this afternoon. "And then right before I came inside he asked if I wanted to go on a date with him. I kinda really want to say yes, but at the same time that scares me...."

"Well, that does sound like you have had an amazing day

Rose. Why don't we start at the beginning and work our way through it?" I nod and she continues, "The first thing I want to go over is Kat coming home. When we spoke previously, you were really worried that you had lost your best friend. Do you still feel that way?"

"Kat coming home was really scary, I can't say it wasn't. Hell, Harrison stayed with me the entire day yesterday helping me prep the apartment and keeping me calm. But as soon as she walked in the door, the fear kinda just poofed. I know she's not the same as she was before, but that's okay. She is still my person." I pause and take a moment to make sure I say what's on my heart the right way, "Trust me, I'm under no delusions that she is back to normal, or that she will be anytime soon. But just having her back is enough for now. I don't think even I realized just how much her being gone and unavailable was messing with me."

Jas is sitting across from me taking notes, but I can tell she isn't surprised by what I've told her. "You don't seem surprised by that." It's a statement more than a question, but she nods anyway.

"That's because I'm not, Rose. You and Kat have formed a bond that is on par with sisters. Like sisters y'all are each other's confidants, partners in life, and each other's constants. You watched that sister implode before your eyes and that terrified you, because there was nothing you could do to fix it yourself. Then you had that same person tell you that you betrayed them by trying to get them the help they needed, right before they had to disconnect from the world. It's only natural that your 'being' in a sense would be off without her.

Now that she is home, your fear is able to relax. You can see with your own eyes that she is okay."

Jas has a look on her face that says she's not done. "You love with your whole heart, Rose, and Kat is a huge part of your heart. You are also a 'fixer', meaning you feel like you have to help with other people's problems. That drive is even stronger with people you deem as 'yours'. Now that she is home, you can see that you made the right call by asking her aunt to take her in. It would never have mattered how much anyone told you that it was the right call. Until you were able to see that it helped her for yourself, in your mind you failed her."

My jaw feels like it is all the way on the floor with her last statement. I hadn't thought about it that way, but she's right. I was constantly worried about Kat while she was gone. Always thinking that I made things worse. It wasn't until she hugged me yesterday that I felt that weight lift. Jaw agape, I chuckle out, "Damn, Jas, you didn't have to attack me like that..."

Jas lets out a full belly laugh. Catching her breath, she says, "That's kinda my job." Pausing, she takes a few more notes. "Now tell me about this Luther fella you mentioned. Is this the same Luther from the coffee shop?"

I feel my mouth tip up in a bit of a smirk, "One and the same." I can feel my face heating at just the thought of him. Staring at my lap, I continue, "We ran into each other again at F.O.U.R.S., turns out he is one of the owners of the club."

Jas lets out a small gasp of surprise, causing me to lift my head. "Wait, do you mean to tell me that not only did you go to the club, which I'm very proud of you for doing by the way and we will come back to that, but that you also ran into your Luther there?"

I beam at her praise, and can't stop the smile that takes over my face as I nod. "And not only was he your Luther from the coffee shop, but none other than Luther Breedlove, club owner and owner of Blackout Distributing?"

The smile on my face is so big it almost hurts, "Well look at you, using your listening ears," I chuckle. "Come to find out he and Harrison are long time acquaintances. When we got to the club, I was still really on edge. Harrison black charmed me to help me feel more comfortable. While we were sitting in the bar, Luther came over to talk to Harrison and formally introduce himself to me. Harrison in-betweened for a bit, but then I decided to ask to just go for it. Let's just say we had a REALLY good night." The smirk that crosses Jas's face isn't lost on me while I'm giving her the high level version of that night.

"I actually know Luther. He's a really great guy, and a fantastic Dom. You mentioned he asked you out but you're afraid to say yes. Why is that?" Taking a deep breath, I try to figure out how to best explain my fears.

"So, we played together a little at the club Friday night, and I'm not sure how or why, but I just felt so comfortable with him from the beginning. And since Friday night we've been texting nonstop. He is so sweet, and thoughtful, and attentive...he even went as far as to check in with me multiple times yesterday, because he knew I was nervous about Kat coming home."

Jas waves her hand in a keep going gesture, so taking another deep breath I continue, "but now he's asking me out on an actual date and I'm terrified of saying yes. All I can think is what if I like him more than he likes me? What if he does like me just as much as I like him, but I'm not what he is looking for? But most of all, what if I give this man my heart and he shatters it?" Damn, I sound like a weak teenager, I feel the first tear roll down my cheek, but keep pushing forward, "He is way out of my league, and I don't think I would survive falling for someone and not being enough for them again."

Jas flips her curls before looking me in the eyes, "Listen Rose, you will always struggle with feeling if you are enough for someone else, if you hold yourself back. The voice in your mind that sounds a lot like your mother telling you, 'you're not beautiful enough, not skinny enough, and that no one will ever want you,' is a lie. I know it was driven even deeper into your mind when you were dating Emily, but those were her insecurities she was projecting onto you."

Just hearing that name forces shivers down my spine, "That feeling that everyone is going to leave because, 'you weren't even enough for your father to show up', can only be demolished by giving someone the opportunity to show you that you are worth showing up for."

She reaches out and grabs my hand, "I know Luther, and putting personal opinions aside, I believe that taking this step with him would be good for you. This may never form into something forever and that's okay. But letting the 'what ifs' cloud your mind could be what stops you from growing and moving towards what could be a beautiful thing." Grabbing a tissue off the table she hands it to me. I didn't even realize I was crying again.

Wiping my eyes does little to slacken the flow of tears falling from my eyes. Squeezing my hand again in hers, she says, "You've already conquered one of your fears this week by going back to the club. I don't even feel like I need to ask you how that went. I can tell just by your body language. Why not take another leap?" Biting her lip, she takes a minute to get her thoughts in order. "You believe in signs right?" I don't even attempt to speak, instead choosing to just nod. "What is more of a sign than running into the guy that inspired your sass to start making an appearance again after one meeting at a coffee shop. Not exchanging information, and then running into him again, at a club specifically for people in the lifestyle?"

Huffing because I know she's right, I blurt out my next thought. "But he's a Daddy Dom! He said he isn't into age play, but I've never been with a Daddy. Hell, I've never even scened with a Daddy! I have no idea what it entails! What if I do something wrong? I'm a brat! Not a Little or a Princess, but a full blown, pain in the ass, needy BRAT! He might not even want that!"

Shaking her head at me she snickers under her breath. "There you go with the 'what ifs' again, Rose. If you're curious and want answers from an outside source, do what you love to do, read a book or two. It's not like there are any shortages of Daddy books out there."

We lock eyes, and she raises her eyebrow in that 'listen and listen well' way that all Tops seem to possess, "As for you being a brat, which, sweets, is beyond obvious, you won't know if that is a dynamic he is interested in consenting to unless you follow the very first rule of kink...hmmm. Remind me what that is again?"

Rolling my eyes, I groan. In the most petulant tone I can conjure while still tearing up, "Ughhh, COMMU-NICATION."

CHAPTER 18

LUTHER

*D*id she really leave me hanging like that? The Little Minx is already bratting and we haven't even gone on a date, yet. I love it. What I don't love though is being left in suspense. I can hope she is feeling the same connection I am but I really have no way to be sure. *Well there's no point in staring at your phone, you dutz. She's in therapy, she isn't going to text you back anytime soon.* Locking my phone, I turn to my computer. *Might as well get some work done.*

I get exactly one and a half emails in before there's a knock on my door. "Come in!" My door swings in with a flourish. I don't even need to look up to see who it is. Leaning back in my chair, I smile up at my head of marketing. "Good afternoon, Nyla! Lovely as always." Scoffing and rolling her eyes at me she practically throws herself on to the couch in my office. *Looks like I'm going to be getting some unexpected entertainment today.* "With that amount of dramatic flare, I know this is going to be good. What's going on?"

Rolling her head to look at me, she lets out what I think is supposed to be a growl. "My damn assistant is absolutely useless! My schedule is an absolute mess, my appointments are all out of order, POs that need attention are scattered everywhere, and she can never get my coffee order right!" Forcing herself to sit up, she turns towards me, "but can I do anything about it? NO! According to HR, I have to give her three written warnings before I'm able to put in the request to fire her. Oh and I can only put in one warning a week! So what? I'm just supposed to have chaos for another two weeks? If it wasn't for my team, I would be drowning by this point!"

Running my hand down my face, I tell her, "The release policies are there to cover our asses. So I can't do much about those. What do you suggest we do?"

"Yeah, yeah I know. I need a new assistant though. Could I at least start interviewing now? It's not like I don't already know she has got to go! She is a twenty year old, social media influencer who has openly admitted that the only reason she is working here is to learn 'how to market herself'. She has been here for two months, and right now the only thing she's marketing herself as is dead weight." Putting her face down in her hands, her "I can't handle this for another two weeks" comes out in a mumble.

Nyla rarely complains about anything, let alone is at a loss to find a solution. In the last ten years we've worked together, I think I have only heard her this desperate once. "Let me talk to Janet, if nothing else, I'll request she be moved up here for now. Flo's last day is Wednesday, so I'll have an opening. But...if I take her, you have to take the assistant that I was about to send an offer to. Deal?"

Nyla, being the ball of barely contained energy that she is, bounces herself to standing. "Really! You would do that for me?" Smiling, I nod. "Is this other assistant any good?"

Raising my brow, I take a moment to answer, "Not that I think you should look a gift horse in the mouth, but yes she is. Her name is Jamie, I'm sure you've met her before. She's Adolfo's daughter. Since HippieHollow burned down she needs a job. She has been running their books and systems since she was eighteen."

Clapping, Nyla squeaks, "Thank you, thank you, thank you! I promise to be nice. If I remember correctly, she frequents the same 'store' we do?" Huffing, I give her a look that I hope screams 'don't go there'. Frequenting the same 'store' as us is our code when we want to verify that someone we know is also a member of the club. Most of my employees aren't members so we try to not talk about it at all. "Listen, she does go to the same store, but she only shops on certain aisles. Don't bring up her special diet unless she does."

She nods her head so fast I'm worried she's going to get whiplash. "No problem, boss! Thank you, again! Let me know what Janet says, and I promise I'll treat the girl right."

My phone starts vibrating just as Nyla is finishing her sentence. Looking over at it, I see it's a new message from Rose. Picking it up with a smile I look back up at Nyla, "Anything else, you freakin' tornado?"

"Umm, yeah. You could tell me who just texted you! I haven't seen you light up like that...well ever..."

"Good Night, Nyla. It's after five. Time for you to head home."

Tossing her head back she saunteers out of the door, whispering under her breath, "Damn spoil sport."

> ROSE
> Sorry for having to run away so quickly earlier. I had therapy… I just got done.

> ME
> That's okay Darlin'.
> I apologize if I came on too strong or made you believe that I had an interest in another woman.

> ROSE
> No you didn't come off too strong! I did think you meant someone else though…and if you did, I mean I get it. I won't be offended.

Leaning back in my chair, I get comfortable. *Oh, my sweet girl, how can I make you understand that you have taken over all of my thoughts. There wouldn't be space enough for another woman even if I wanted there to be. Which I don't...*

> ME
> Darlin' let me make something very clear to you…

> I am not nor do I want to be courting anyone else. I have been single for three years and in that time I have only gone on two actual dates. Neither of which I actually wanted to go on.
>
> Meeting you has sparked something in me and I would like to explore it.

My chest is tight by the time I'm done typing. I can't remember the last time I was that vulnerable with someone. The last woman I let really see me, ripped my heart into pieces. If I'm honest with myself, I don't remember ever even feeling this strongly for her. Especially this early on. It doesn't matter, I've put myself out there now. Either I just completely blew my chance with this woman, or we are set up for one hell of an adventure.

ROSE
> Damn it! I thought I was done with crying today. That was incredibly sweet.
>
> I really like you too Luther. I won't lie to you, but that scares me.

ME
> Well if you'll let me I would love to earn your trust Darlin'.
>
> How can help ease your fears?

ROSE
> IDK honestly. I'm a lot to deal with Luther. Too much if I'm being totally blunt. I don't know that I'll be someone you want.

My hackles raise when I read her text. Who made her

feel like she was too much? I have to be careful with how I respond.

> **ME**
> Darlin' I don't know who has made you feel like you're too much and I know I don't have the right to ask yet. However, what I can tell you if that if you give me chance I will work to earn that right. I will work to tear down those walls I can see you've built around your heart.

*I really hope that didn't come off as corny...*I meant every word, though. Even if we don't happen to work together, I'm going to make sure this woman learns her worth.

> **ROSE**
> Yes

> **ME**
> Yes? Yes to what?

> **ROSE**
> Yes Luther, I'll go out with you.

> **ME**
> Wednesday?

> **ROSE**
> I work on Wednesday.

> **ME**
> I do too. What time do you get off?

> **ROSE**
> Whenever you get me off 😉

She is so damn adorable. I love it when she shows me her sass...I'll love it even more when I can play with it.

> **ME**
> Well I have to at least buy you dinner first... I am a gentleman like that.

> **ROSE**
> A gentleman indeed. I should get off no later than 5:30. It won't take me long to get home.

> **ME**
> Perfect, how about I pick you up at 7? Or would you and Kat feel more comfortable with you meeting me there?

> **ROSE**
> Oh you're good... I'm okay with you picking me up, but let me ask Kat if she comfy with that.

> **ME**
> I'm looking forward to it Darlin'!

Tapping my phone on my chin, I start to work up a plan. This beautiful woman doesn't seem to see herself. Guess it'll be my job to show her just how special she is. Smirking to myself, I send one more text.

> **ME**
> Hey Harrison. It's Luther. I need your help with something.

CHAPTER 19

ROSE

*H*aving Monday off to spend with Kat was great and all, but catching up on tasks that I normally do, SUCKS. I spent all day yesterday organizing the pick-up schedules, figuring out if we have enough cars to get us through the week, dealing with adjusters, and attempting to track down repo vehicles that should have already been dropped off. I got it done, but it was exhausting.

Today has been much better. Everyone is actually here, and from what I can tell our driver facing team is actually doing what they are supposed to do. It's a rare day indeed around here, and I know better than to say anything to jinx it. I'm leaning back in my chair daydreaming when Bruce walks in the office. "Whatcha doin'? He asks me, pulling me out of my thoughts. "What?" I ask. He chuckles at me, knowing I wasn't paying a bit of attention, "I asked you what you were doin'? You looked like you were lost in space."

"Well, I was...obviously...," I sass, rolling my eyes at him. He raises his brow at me before responding, "Alright, sassy pants," *crap he is gonna keep digging and he has 'I'm in charge' tone going.* "What were you thinking about? And don't try and give me any crap about it not being anything, or that it was about work."

Turning to him fully, I shoot a pout his way. "You know it isn't fair that you can do that. You shouldn't be able to read me that well." *Am I really that transparent?*

Sitting in one of the other office chairs, he smirks at me. "I'm not only your friend, which means I know you, but I'm also a Dom. Reading cues and body language is what I do. Now, quit stalling. What's going on?"

I let out a dramatic sigh before I give in and answer him. "Urg, you're a pain!" Tossing my head backwards, I let it all out, "Fine, I have a date tonight. I was sitting here freaking out about it. I'm nervous and I don't even know what to wear! Like, I haven't dated anyone since Emily, and even then I planned everything. I don't even have an idea of where we are going tonight!"

The room is oddly quiet when I'm done with my little freak-out rant. When I finally bring myself to lower my head, I'm surprised to see not only an irritated look on Bruce's face, but Matt standing just inside the doorway looking just as grumpy. "Oh, hey Matt. I didn't hear you come in, everything okay? You look like someone pissed in your coffee."

Moving fully in the room, Matt closes the office door and takes a seat before addressing my question. *Shit, did I mess something up?* "Not funny, Rose. What is this about dating and not knowing where y'all are going? That isn't the safest move, girly. How did y'all meet? Do you even know this guy?

Why is this the first time we are hearing about this?" His voice is almost at a full blown growl.

Throwing my hands up to get him to stop for a second, I look over at Bruce. "Umm, a little help here?"

Giving me an evil smirk, Bruce shakes his head. "Why would I help, Rose, when I want to know the same things?" His voice sounds tight, like he is trying to hold his anger back. *I wonder if he knows he's failing...MISERABLY.*

Ugghhh! "I don't know why you two are so upset. It isn't like you're the one going on the date!" *Stupid guy alpha moments,* I couldn't stop the eyeroll I send their way even if I wanted to. Using my fingers to list off the answers they are damn near demanding, I snap, "To answer your questions, I'm going on a first date. I don't know where we are going because he said he would send me the address an hour before. We met for the first time at the coffee shop. I've been talking to him for about a week, but Harrison has known him for a while. And this is the first time you're hearing about it because I knew you would go all grumpy protective older brother on me! Like you are right now!"

It's clear they both still have questions, but at least they don't look like they are ready to attack anymore. Matt is the first one to say anything, "I'm sorry for jumping down your throat, Rose. It's just we care about you and we saw just how bad that bitch fucked you up. We don't want you to go through that again."

Bruce runs his hand down his face before he picks up where Matt left off. "I'm not going to discourage you from going, because I know Harrison would never knowingly let you go out with someone if he thought they would hurt you. I am, however, going to be checking up on you. Would you be willing to text us where y'all are going tonight when you find out?" The little smile he gives me when he asks is adorable. I love these guys. They might be over the top, but I know it's just because they care.

I give them both a shy smile. *Rose, if you don't, they are liable to just show up to the apartment.* Exhaling, I give them what they want. "Okay, okay. I'll send you the info when I have it. Not like y'all couldn't just track me with FindOntheGo anyways." My phone dings on my desk but I ignore it for now. "I'm sorry that I sent y'all into worry-about-me mode." I really am, I don't need them to worry about me.

Bruce's face and voice are soft when he speaks again. "There is no need to be sorry, Rose. We just want you safe and happy. Just don't make us have to go to jail to do it, miss ma'am." I chuckle at that. "What's his name?"

I feel a wide grin take over my face, "His name is Luther, he is really kind, and he owns not only one business, but two." I take a second to decide how I want to continue, "We've been talking constantly and I don't know, he's just made me feel super comfortable with him. Jas knows him, too, and she believes this might be a good step for me."

For just a moment I see shock and recognition cross Bruce's face, but just as fast as it's there it's gone. I can see the question in his eye, but I know he won't ask it in front of Matt. I give him a quick nod to answer his unspoken question. *Yes, he's in the lifestyle too.*

Walking into the apartment after work, I try to calm my jitters. Kat's sitting on our couch with her laptop in front of her looking comfy. I must startle her when I drop my things on the counter, because she jumps and squeals like a little mouse. Turning to me, her face is scrunched up and disgruntled, "GEEEZ, ROSE, ARE YOU TRYING TO GIVE ME A HEART ATTACK?" Her voice cracks as she squeaks out her disapproval.

Giggling, I skip over to the couch and flop down. "I'm sorry, I didn't mean to scare you by daring to come home to our apartment on time." Tackling her down onto the cushion, I beg, "Could you ever forgive me, oh bestie of mine?"

Kat bursts out into a fit of giggles, too, hollering, "GET OFF OF ME! YOU BIG ASS BRAT! GET OFF!" *Oh she wants a brat I'll give her a brat.* I start tickling her wildly. "OH, MY GOSH, ROSE! NO! STOP IT! THAT'S SO NOT FAIR!" Tears run down both of our cheeks. We are laughing so hard. She keeps trying to tickle me back but can't seem to manage it. *Score for me!* "ROSE! CUT IT OUT OR I'M GONNA PEE!!!" My hands immediately fly in the air. I know Kat and if she says she will pee, then her hydrant is ready to burst. Been there, done that, threw away the outfit.

As soon as I am out of her way, Kat springs up and takes off running for the bathroom. "You jerk! I don't even have panties on!" she squeals. Another round of giggles breaks out of me, sending me backwards towards the floor. I land with an UMPH. I yell back at her, "DON'T WORRY, I'D FALL FOR YOU ALL OVER AGAIN!"

I've finished my hair and make up, and now I'm standing at my closet door debating what the hell I'm gonna wear.

Grabbing my phone I send a quick text to Harrison,

> **ME**
> UGHH!! I wish you were here. I have no clue what to wear!!

> **HARRISON**
> Well, I guess you should open your door then.

I rush to the door and check the peephole before flinging it open. "What are you doing here?" I say excitedly. Both Harrison and Kat start laughing. "Let the man in, Rose!" I hear from the kitchen. Waving Harrison in, I shut and lock the door back. He turns on me immediately with a tick in his jaw. "Well, who pissed in your cheerios?" I ask him in a sassy tone, "I was excited to see you, but I'm not so sure now.".

"Rose Marie Morrow...why in the hell are you opening the door in your underwear?" He growls at me. I look down and realize that just like he said...I'm in nothing but my pretty black lace bra and pantie set. *Well, shit.* "Um, I'm going to blame Kat," I hear a "HEY" come from the kitchen but keep going, "for making the temperature in this apartment so warm. I didn't realize I never put any of the outfits I put together in my head, actually on my body." I give him the most innocent 'please don't yell at me' look I can muster.

Kat steps out and comes to my rescue, "At least it was just Harrison. Not like he hasn't seen you in less." She turns and looks me up and down, "You look hot as hell babe, but I don't think that outfit is appropriate for a public first date." I can't even with her so I just roll my eyes and turn back to Harrison. I've barely met his eyes before she pipes up again, "OOOHHHH, you brought presents!"

Harrison chuckles and shakes his head at her antics. "I did, however they aren't from me." Both of us look at him with confusion. Instead of elaborating on what he means by that, he hands Kat a small gift bag. Kat being one to never question a gift, squeaks and immediately opens it. When she opens the small box held inside she gasps. Pulling out a dainty gold necklace with a pretty lavender flower encased in glass as a pendant. It is absolutely beautiful. Harrison then hands her a card. "This goes with it." Smiling, he looks at me and continues, "These bags here are for you, BooBear." I'm shocked speechless, but there's no need to say anything since he also hands me a card. "Card first, then open."

A sniffle from next to us catches our attention, Kat has tears running down her smiling face. She looks up at me, but says nothing, just hands me the card in her hand.

Kat,

I hope this letter finds you well. My name is Luther, and I will be the one taking your best friend on a date this evening. That however is not why I wanted to send you this small token.

I have heard of the disgusting incident that happened to you and am appalled by it. I know my opinion neither matters, nor will it change the facts, but I wanted you to know nonetheless.

In regards to the necklace, lavender in the flower world represents three things: Peace, Healing, and Strength. I hope this pendant brings you a sense of all of these on days when you are struggling.

I also want to give you one other thing. If you ever decide you

> want to try within the lifestyle again. You have a permanent VIP membership to F.O.U.R.S.
> Again, this has nothing to do with me dating Rose. This is something myself and the other owners spoke about prior. We want to make sure you always have a safe space to go and be your freest self. No strings attached.
> Sending you thoughts and strength,
> Luther M. Breedlove

Oh, my sweetness. I feel my own tears starting to pool in my eyes as I come to the end of the letter. Looking up at Harrison he gives me the smallest smirk. "He asked me to deliver since I was bringing yours," he says, then nods down at the envelope still in my hand, "Read it."

> *Darlin'*
> I hope this letter finds you as excited for tonight as I am.. I had a feeling that since you don't know exactly where we are going tonight, picking out an outfit would be difficult, so I enlisted some assistance. Harrison has picked out 2 outfits for you to choose from since he knows your style. Yes, I know I'm over the top, but I want to show you just how special you truly are.
>
> *I'll see you soon,*
> Hopefully your soon-to-be Daddy

I jerk up to meet Harrison's eyes, gasping out, "You

sneaky man! You didn't!" Winking at me he replies, "Oh, I did. Now come on, you don't have a lot of time to get ready."

Harrison turns me towards our room smacking my ass as I move forward. "Hey!" I holler, the impact leaving an unexpected sting. "You're lucky that's all you're gettin', girl. Even if it was just me at the door, opening the door in nothin' but this sexy little number is a crime," he reprimands. Snatching my note out of my hand Kat reads it out. "Damn Girl! I like Daddy! You can keep him!" Me and Harrison burst out laughing, I try to look at her with a sour face but can't hide my smile when I say, "Don't call him Daddy, he's mine."

Luther was spot on, Harrison brought two completely different options. Option one is a royal blue knee length bodycon dress with a square neck and cap sleeves. It's absolutely stunning and I think I have the perfect accessories to go with it. Option two are dark green high waisted sailor trousers with gold buttons on the top and a cream off the shoulder top. "Damn, Harrison! You're two for two! Both outfits are amazing! Um, but how am I supposed to choose?" I ask with both awe and confusion.

Smiling down at me he brushes a curl off my face before saying, "Go with the dress, that's my favorite. Plus, that color will look fantastic on you." Shyly, I bring myself to ask, "Is this weird for you? I mean I know we've...and you like him... and now..." He places his hand over my mouth to shut me up. "BooBear, you are one of my best friends. Yes, we have fucked, but no I'm not jealous, I just..." He trails off, I can see the wheels in his mind turning, before I can say anything he continues, "I'm not sure what I feel for Luther. Is he a buddy? Yeah. Do I like him as a friend? Yes. But am I looking at pursuing something with him? I don't think so. I mean don't get me wrong, if the opportunity to play together came up, I don't think I'd say no, but that's about it. I've never been attracted to any man in any sort of way before, so why would I go from zero to sixty?"

Looking into his eyes, I see the truth behind his words. "Promise me you'll tell me if it starts to be?" I ask. His eyes sparkle with what I can only call love. "Promise, Boo Bear."

CHAPTER 20

LUTHER

My nerves are going insane, I want tonight to go off without a hitch. Harrison told me she likes Italian food, so I chose 'La Sinfonia' for tonight. The quaint little restaurant is nice for a first date, but not over the top. With only around thirty tables in the restaurant, you can actually hear the other person you're with. Five minutes before our meeting time, I get out of my vehicle to stand near the entrance. *Please let this go well.*

Rose is all I can see the moment she steps out of her car. It's almost as if she is glowing. The dress she's wearing caresses her curves in a way that can only be described as sinful. Paired with a sexy as hell pair of black strappy heels and I'm a goner. *Note to self, send Harrison a thank you gift.* As she approaches me, I see the trepidation in her eyes, even through the smile she has on her face. I can't help but wonder what has her fearful at this moment.

"Good evening, Luther," she says. The sound of my name

on her lips sends shivers down my spine all over again. "I hope you haven't been waiting long." She fidgets with her hands, looking a bit sheepish. *Nope, can't have that.* I gently take her hand and bring it to my lips. Kissing the back before greeting her, "Good evening, Darlin'. You look stunning."

A slight flush takes over her features at my compliment. My mind flashes back to the night at the club. The sheen of heat on her skin, the way her face morphed with pleasure, the breathy way she moaned when she was overwhelmed. *Get it together Luther! You are supposed to be a gentleman tonight!* I can't bring myself to let go of her hand. Her touch alone sends electricity down my spine and it is intoxication in its purest form. "Shall we go eat, Darlin'?" She gives me the most adorable little nod, before she responds, "I think we should, I'm famished."

Since we came in the middle of the week, there are only 4 other tables currently occupied. Rose is looking around in awe as we are led back to our table. "This place is beautiful, Luther. How did you find it?" Smiling at the memory, I pull out her chair. "Lets order first and then I'll take you down memory lane."

The waiter who brought us to our table, waits patiently while I take a seat and then asks for our drink orders. Glancing over at Rose, I can see she isn't quite ready. Understandable, since she hasn't been here before. Nodding at the waiter, I tell him, "Can we get some water for now please. I would like to make sure I pair the wine with what we order this evening."

"You already knew what you wanted, didn't you?" she

asks as soon as the waiter walks away. "Yeah, but you don't and I don't know about you, but I am in no hurry for tonight to end." I watch her lift her menu up just enough to cover her mouth. "Thank you, I really do suck at decision making sometimes. Especially under pressure, I don't usually have that issue at work. There I just do, you know? But outside of work, it's like I just can't do it half the time." She's doing that nervous rambling thing again. As adorable as it is, I don't want her to feel uncomfortable here or with me.

Taking her menu from her and setting it down on the table, I wait until her eyes meet mine. I might be wrong about what she needs but I don't believe I am. When she finally meets my eyes, I jump in head first, "Then you don't need to make a decision, Darlin'. Let me take over for now. All I need is for you to tell me if there is anything you don't like or are allergic to."

I can see both the acceptance and mischief in her eyes, "Well, since we are talking about dislikes and allergies, I strongly dislike veggies and water and I'm extremely allergic to toxic bs." She winks at me, "But since I don't see any of that here, please proceed with your takeover, because I have nooo idea what's good here."

She's sassing me. I never thought I could feel so much happiness hearing sass coming from a woman's mouth.

"Alright, sassy pants, I'm going to take that to mean you don't have any real food allergies that I need to be worried about. Am I right?" She giggles and nods her head. "Do you like lamb?" The sound that comes out of this woman's mouth is more mouth watering than anything they could possibly serve on the menu. "I love lamb. I haven't had it in years though." Nodding, I set our menus down toward the front of the table, signaling to the waiter we are ready to order.

As expected, he wastes no time coming over. "What can I get y'all this evening?" The waiter looks to take her order first and it isn't until she nods towards me that he changes his attention. "We will take a bottle of the house Merlot, and the Bruschetta flight and Fritto Misto to start. For the main course, we would like the Roast lamb Risotto, and the Spaghetti alla puttanesca." He reviews our order and I thank him before he heads back to the kitchen.

Smiling when I turn back to Rose, I take a moment to get my senses about me. She's letting me take the lead tonight and I refuse to take that for granted. "You promised me a story, sir," she says to me with just the slightest hint of sass. "That I did, my dear," I say, "This restaurant has been here for almost sixty years. Nonna Gianna and Nonno Alessio were both second generation immigrants and wanted to prove themselves to their families. So, after they got married, they moved here from New York. They worked their tails off and opened this restaurant. My grandpa was a chef and when they were looking for help he came and worked here. Grandpa and Nonno became friends quickly and as soon as Gran and Nonna met, they were attached at the hip. My mom grew up coming here and then, when I was little, we used to come here every other Sunday after church."

Some of my fondest memories have happened in this place, but I don't want to overwhelm her. The lightness of her voice is soothing, "Please go on, I can tell there's more," she urges. I smile and let myself get lost in the story "Nonna was actually the one to give me my first job. She brought new hire paperwork in a gift box to my fifteenth birthday dinner," Rose giggles, "I was a host for the first year and then, when I turned sixteen, I started waiting tables. Their daughter and her husband were killed in a car accident that year, and it almost destroyed them." Rose lets out a quiet gasp so I reach out and squeeze her hand.

"My parents and a few of their other close friends stepped in to keep this place going. It took almost a year before either one of them could come in and actually be here. I have always seen them as an additional set of grandparents and they have always treated me like I was theirs. I truly believe they are the ones who gave me the drive to own my own business."

The waiter comes over with our wine then, saving me from continuing on with my story. I would hate to ruin this date with me going on and on. Taking a sip of my wine, I gesture towards her, "Okay, enough about me, tell me about you, Rose. Did you grow up in Texas?"

She winces a little before squaring her shoulders. "No, I grew up in a small town in Missouri. I only moved here a little under 3 years ago. I couldn't stand the idea of going back to living under a microscope; so, when I finished college, I moved here."

Her face morphs into a mixture of both fear and disgust when she mentions living under a microscope, I can't just let that go. "So you didn't like living in such a small town?" She clears her throat before speaking again, "Something like that," she fidgets with her glass and takes a sip. "When you live in a small town, everyone knows everyone. The gossip is rampant, and there is just no privacy. You add that in with my parents controlling nature and you end up under a magnifying glass anywhere you go. My mom got even worse my sophomore year, after my dad divorced her for one of his clients. I knew if I went back now it would only get worse."

"Why's that?" I ask. She lets out a small huff, "I really don't think you want to know that." I wink at her, but before I can speak, our antipasti is being set in front of us. "Thank you," I say to our waiter. As soon as he steps away, I address her again, "I promise, you won't scare me." She's looking down at the food instead of at me, but I can tell this is something that really bothers her. "If you don't want to talk about it, Darlin', you don't have to."

I watch her take a deep breath before she brings her eyes to meet mine. "I've always been a bigger girl and my mom didn't like that. When I lived at home, she would monitor everything I ate. In middle school and beginning of high school, it was mostly keeping me from eating junk food and her making comments meant to cut. When my dad left, it changed to keeping me on a really strict diet. If she even heard about me going somewhere that she didn't approve of, there were...consequences."

The more she speaks, the more my blood boils. *How could someone treat their own daughter that way!* She's not finished yet, and I know deep down this is only scratching the surface. "I haven't been home since the summer after my freshman year of college. I've avoided that place like the plague, since I'm bigger now than I was then." Seeing she needs a break from the topic, I ask, "So, why Austin?"

The smile that takes over her face is electrifying. Just seeing it light up her face calms my anger and I'm excited to hear what put it there. "That's easy. I moved here because of Harrison." I feel a twinge of jealousy at just how much happiness just the thought of him seems to bring her, but I quickly tamp it down. *They are just friends.* I tell myself. *Friends that fuck, but they both already told you it's nothing more than that.* "Harrison moved into our neighborhood during our sophomore year. He was super sweet and kinda shy, so me and Kat kinda, I don't know adopted him? He was a Senior, but the older kids already had their groups. So he was...just ours. When he left for school we all stayed in touch and then, when it was time for me and Kat to pick schools, we decided to go where he went. As soon as we got to Dallas, he took us in and showed us the ropes. Mom was happy I'd have a man to look after me and I was happy to have my friend. When we graduated, it was an easy choice for me on where to move."

Our food is brought to the table, essentially halting our conversation. Served family style with the food in the middle and us each having our own individual plates. I raise and grab her plate, causing her to look at me confused. "You are a queen, Darlin', you should always be served when possible." She looks shocked, but I choose not to comment on it. Giving her a decent helping of both dishes, I place her plate back in front of her and peck her temple. Rounding to my side of the table, I sit and serve myself.

"Thank you, Luther. That was beyond kind of you." She says, still looking like she doesn't know how to react. "You're very welcome, Darlin', just being respectful. My momma would tan my hide if I didn't treat a queen as she deserves."

She takes her first bite of risotto and moans. The sound shooting straight to my cock. "Oh my God, this is

BREATHE

SOOOOOO GOOOOODDDD. She says with an almost orgasmic sigh. She tries the meat next and lets out another. My cock is hard as steel in my pants. The blood flowing there so fast, I'm lightheaded. I want to hear her make those sounds while she's underneath me. So intoxicated on pleasure and sensations, she can't tell where one ends and the other begins. "Darlin', as much as I love to hear your sounds of pleasure, I'm trying to be a gentleman." I tell her. She looks me right in the eye as she tries the chicken and does it again.

The rest of our meal goes by pretty uneventfully. She only finishes about half of her food, before she proclaims she's stuffed. She stares at it like it's done something wrong, so I ask, "Did the food anger you in some way?" Her body language screams sass when she responds. "Actually, it's more my stomach. I'm mad there isn't more room in it. The food was just that good." I chuckle, "I'll get it boxed up for you to take home. It'll be alright." She beams up at me. Just knowing I put that smile on her face makes me feel ten feet tall. I catch the eye of our waiter and motion towards the plates to let him know we are ready for boxes. As soon as I see him head into the kitchen, I already know what's coming. *Dammit, I didn't know she was here tonight...*

Giving Rose a nervous smile, I quickly say, "I would like to apologize now for the embarrassment that is about to happen." She doesn't have a chance to even ask me what I mean before we hear, "Il mio bellissimo nipote" booming from the kitchen doorway.

Nonna struts over to our table like she's on her own personal catwalk. Pink glitter cane and all. I stand to greet her, and she hugs me like she didn't just see me at Sunday dinner. "Nonna, I didn't know you were working tonight. It's so good to see you." The moment I say Nonna, recognition flashes across Rose's face. Before she can shrink back into herself I reach out for her. "Nonna, this is Rose. Rose, this is Nonna Gianna."

CHAPTER 21

ROSE

Don't panic, don't panic, DO NOT PANIC! Standing when Luther reaches over to me, I try not to let my fear win. "Nonna, this is Rose. Rose, this is Nonna Gianna." Luther says to her. "Hello ma'am, it's lovely to meet you." I greet her. "Sit, sit," she tells us. My eyes don't leave Luther as he moves towards her again, and pulls out her chair. Once he has her settled, he walks behind me to help me scoot forward. Leaning in close, he whispers in my ear, "Darlin', I know this was unexpected for both of us, but everything will be just fine." Before he pulls back completely, he squeezes my shoulder and lays a small kiss on my temple. *Why do I love it when he does that so much?*

Nonna is watching us the entire time and I can see the smile behind her eyes. I feel the tension rush out of me. I'm not positive how he did it, but just in that small gesture, Luther has managed to both calm my racing heart and ignite it at the same time. He returns to his seat and sends me a devilish wink, before turning to his Nonna.

"How did you enjoy your meal, Rose?" She asks me. "Oh, it was fantastic. I can honestly say I think it was the best Italian I've ever had." I chuckle out. Giving me the most adorable shy smirk, she says. "Oh well, I'm glad you enjoyed it. I wouldn't say it's the best, but I'm no slouch in the kitchen." She's trying to play coy, but Luther isn't having it. "Nonna, she was out here scowling at her food because she was full, but didn't want to stop eating." My jaw drops, I wasn't lying when I said it was the best I've ever had, but he didn't have to throw me under the bus like that.

"A woman after my own heart. I hate it when I'm forced to end something I find pleasurable." She says it in such a way that it's clear she meant the double meaning. Luther's jaw hangs wide at her comment, while Gianna just winks at me. *Okay, Nonna. Looks like you love the shock factor too.* I beam at her, the fact that she just went out of her way to push back at him means a lot.

"So tell me, how long have you two been together?" She's giving us both a knowing look, but finally settles her eyes on Luther. "Is this the girl you mentioned at dinner?" Luther actually looks shy. Looking at her first before turning to look at me, he replies, "She is, we met a few weeks ago, but this is kind of our first date." We both look at her, but she just grins. "Well then, let me leave you two to it. This old woman needs to get back to work." We both stand when she does, "It was fabulous meeting you, ma'am." She grabs my hand tightly, saying, "None of this ma'am business, it's Nonna. And it was wonderful to meet you, too, Rose." Pulling me closer she hugs me and whispers in my ear, "I like you, don't be a stranger." Releasing me, she turns to

Luther and kisses him on the cheek. "Love you, nipote. Antonio will be out in just a moment to box up the food." Sauntering off towards the kitchen, she says. "You kids have fun!"

Returning to our seats, I can't hold back my giggle. Covering my face with my hands, I say, "Oh my gosh, I can't believe I just met your Nonna." He's quiet, forcing me to pull my face out of my hands. "I really didn't know she was here tonight. Was it too much?" His obvious nerves make me smile. "No, not at all. I really like her. She seems like a feisty one. Plus, I can tell she adores you." His smile reminds me of a young boy as he says, "She's a truly amazing woman."

A few minutes pass while we talk and just get to know each other. "So, you have three siblings?" I ask him. "Ah, you mean three pains in my ass? Yeah, I do," He says, rolling his eyes. "Two brothers and a sister. Xavier who's thirty nine, Kylo who's thirty four, and Aniya is the baby at thirty." That makes me realize I never even asked him his age. "Where do you fall in that mix?" I ask, trying to ask him his age without being rude. "I'm the oldest." He smirks down at me. "Now, ask the question you want to ask, Rose." *Damn, am I that obvious?*

Biting my lip nervously, I mumble, "How old are you?" Apparently though, mumbling won't be accepted here. "What was that?" He asks, "I couldn't understand your little grumble there." *Well, shit.* Taking a calming breath, I look up at him and try again, "How old are you?" He winks at me. "Good Girl, that's better." His words send shivers down my spine. Two little words should not affect me the way they do, but dammit they do. "To answer your question, Darlin', I'm forty two." I'm stunned, I knew he was older than me, but I didn't expect that.

He must be able to tell I'm caught off guard, because he asks, "Does my age bother you, Darlin'?" I try to meet his eyes, but can't seem to do it. I know my voice is quivering when I finally answer. "No, it doesn't bother me. I knew you were older than me going in. I just didn't realize just how wide the gap was. It makes me nervous."

He stands and moves his chair closer to mine. When he sits back down, he's fully facing me. Luther places his finger under my chin and gently lifts my face to his. I still can't look him in the eyes, my mind is starting to spiral and my insecurities come forward. "Eyes on me, Rose," he demands in a tone that is gentle, but still an order. It's something only a true dominant can manage.

Slowly, I bring my eyes to meet his. "That's it, so brave for me. Now tell me, Darlin', why does my age make you so nervous?" My heart starts to race and my eyes flick back and forth between his. He adjusts his hand that is still holding my chin up, and gently squeezes. "You're okay, Darlin'. Take a deep breath for me." My body immediately obeys, there's something about this man that calls to my very soul. Feeling only marginally more centered, I let my words come out in a rush. "I'm scared that you'll think I'm too young for you. I'm only twenty six and that's a huge difference. I like you, a lot, and I don't really know why. I can't even explain it, but I feel safe with you. I don't want to lose that. Don't get me wrong, I would a thousand percent understand and back away quietly if it bothers you. I just want you to..."

He cuts off the words spewing from my mouth by

placing his finger across my lips. "Enough," he says sternly. "Just like you knew I was older than you, I knew you were younger than me. It neither bothers me, nor does it change anything for me. I don't care how many years you have been walking this earth. What I care about is what is in here," he lightly taps my temple, "I care about what makes this keep beating," he lays his hand over my heart before moving to take my hand, "and above all else I care about the person you are."

"You, sir, are too perfect. Like a seriously neon bright green flag." I say while gapping at him. He chuckles at my response, "I'm nowhere near perfect, Darlin'." He glances over my shoulder and lets out another giggle. "I guess Nonna likes you." I turn to look at what's caught his eye. I can't believe what I'm seeing. Our waiter, whose name I guess is Antonio, is carrying two huge bags and is followed by another young woman carrying another large bag and one smaller one. They both stop at the hostess stand and set down the bags. Anonio quickly says something to the hostess then heads our way.

Eyes focused on Luther, Anonio says, "Nonna G told me that I had to tell you, 'Kiss her old ass, dinner's on her'." He then turns to me and continues, "She also told me to tell you that, 'It's a crime to turn food down from an Italian grandmother, she's an old lady and can do what she pleases'. I promise those were her words not mine."

Both Luther and I burst out laughing. "Don't worry Ton' I know Nonna didn't give you much choice." Antonio's whole body relaxes, "One last thing," he says, "she also told me to tell you that the little bag is for you and the other bags are for the pretty lady with you." Luther falls into another fit of laughter, while I'm in complete shock.

Once Luther stops laughing, he reaches for his wallet, "Here Ton' take this. She might be covering dinner but you did a fantastic job. Keep putting the lady first, that's a real man mentality."

Standing, he places a bill in Antonios hand then comes around to me. Taking my hand in his, he helps me stand and leads me towards the door. Antonio follows us and takes the two bags he had originally, while Luther grabs the others. "I'll help you carry these out." I give him a huge smile, "Thank you, Antonio, you really are a gentleman."

The bags are so big that they take up both floorboards and the passenger seat. "Why would she send all this food home with me?" I ask Luther, still in absolute shock that a woman I met for all of five minutes would do something so kind. His eyes sparkle down at me. "Like I said before, Darlin'. She likes you. Trust me, that woman is not afraid to tell anyone what she thinks about them." I blink up at him, "Okay, but why so much?" He chuckles, "Don't worry, Darlin'. You'll get used to people wanting to take care of you soon enough."

Reaching out, he brushes a strand of hair off my face. His voice is almost a growl when he speaks. "I'm going to kiss you now." My heart starts beating rapidly in my chest as he leans in. His eyes never leave mine on his descent. As soon as his lips touch mine, my body erupts in goosebumps. I lean into the kiss, using my body to show him I am okay with where this is going. Taking my cue, he deepens the kiss.

Our tongues dance together, and my body heats. Flashes of our night together play through my mind. His body on mine, the feel of his teeth biting into my flesh. He lets out a deep groan, making my hunger for him grow even more. Sliding my hands up his arms to the back of his neck, I give in to him fully. His hand at the small of my back pulls me in tighter. I can feel how hard he is between us and moan at the feeling. Sliding his other hand from my jaw he tangles it in my hair. *Fucccckkk, I need this man to devour every inch of me.*

    The hand in my hair tightens. He uses the grip to pull my head back, breaking the kiss. For a moment, I'm in a daze wondering why he stopped. Both of us are breathing erratically, the tension in the air thick enough you could cut it with a knife. Luther brings his forehead down to mine. Breaths mingling, I itch to lean up and take his lips with mine again, but I know he pulled back for a reason.

    Luther speaks first, "Darlin', we have to stop. I wouldn't fuck you for the first time in a parking lot. I'm damn sure not going to outside of Nonnas." His words drop me back into our reality. Blinking, I try to move back but he only lets me get a little space between us. My voice is raspy when I speak, "I'm sorry, I forgot where we were for a second." I meet his eyes and smile. "For a second there, I did too, Darlin'." We stand there for another minute just holding each other. "You need to get home, beautiful." Poking my lip out at him, I pout, "What if I don't want to go home?"

    "Minx," or at least I think that's what I hear him call me but it is drowned out by the growl that comes from deep in his chest. "As much as I want to ravage you, I'm not going to. Not tonight, anyways." His words are like an icy wave against my overheated skin, cooling me instantly. I take another step backwards out of his hold. He must finally realize what he said, or at least how I took it because he reaches out and cups my face again.

"Hey," he says in that sexy as hell tone that gets me every time, "let me clarify. I want to be with you, make no mistake about that. It just can't happen tonight. I want to get to know your heart, before I claim your body. I know that sounds ridiculous coming from someone whose whole career is literally based on indulgence." That makes me giggle, "But there's something about you, Darlin'. I don't want to only claim your body. I want to own your soul. Explore this with me, and I'm positive what's between us will be explosive."

"Okay," it's the only word I can get out and even then it comes out weak. "Okay?" He asks. I clear my throat and try again, "Okay, let's explore." The smile that takes over his face is intoxicating. It only lasts for a moment though before it falls into a frown. "Listen, I didn't tell you this before because it wasn't pertinent to the relationship we had. It is now."

Fuck, is he married? No, he can't be, I didn't see a ring on his finger, and Harrison would have told me. He knows I don't do the married thing. Does he have a kid? I mean, if he does that's fine but how would they take this. Rubbing his thumb across my cheek he continues, "Darlin', I can see you over thinking things, but it's nothing bad." I relax under his touch wanting to hear what he needs to tell me. "I'm flying out on business tomorrow and won't be back until the Friday after next. I have a few new distillers to check out and need to check in on my satellite office."

I reach up and smack his chest, "DON'T DO THAT!" I scold. "Do what?" He asks me. I can tell he's trying to hold back his laugh. "Scare me like that! I thought you had like a secret wife or kid. Not a business trip!" Leaning down, he presses a kiss to my forehead. "Darlin', I wouldn't have kept anything like that from you. I'm sorry I scared you."

Shooting him a playful glare, I grumble out a "Thank you". He fixes my hair again before sighing. "We both really should be getting home beautiful. It's getting late." Looking down at my watch I'm shocked to see that it's already almost ten thirty. "Wow you're right," I meet his eyes again, "so, I won't talk to you for two weeks?" He looks at me confused. "What makes you think that?" I shuffle a bit on my feet. "Well, you'll be out of town working. Won't you be busy?" He brushes another small kiss across my lips, "I might be busy, but not too busy to talk to my girl."

With a wink, he reaches behind me and opens the driver door. "Now go, before I change my mind and steal you away." Getting in, I start the car and roll down my window. "Who says you'd have to steal me?" With a laugh he taps the roof of my car. "Good night, Little Minx. Text me when you get home." He takes a step back and I reverse out of my spot. It's just as I put the car in drive to pull away, that I yell out "Night, Daddy!"

CHAPTER 22

ROSE

Twenty minutes later I'm pulling into my parking spot at our apartment. Tonight has me on cloud nine and I don't want to come down. Reaching for my phone, I notice it isn't in the mount like normal. I was so busy replaying tonight in my head, I forgot to even pull it out. Digging through my purse, I find it near the bottom. Unlocking it, I see I have a few missed messages and two missed calls. Ignoring those for now I call Kat. She answers after the second ring, "Do you need a bestie extraction?" I giggle, "No drama queen, come downstairs and help me." I can hear her moving around through the phone. "Help you?" Popping my lips, I say the one thing I know will get her down here no questions asked, "Italian food," and then hang up.

Opening my message app, I roll my eyes. I have messages from Kat, Harrison, Matt, Bruce, Luther, and, ugh, my mother.

KAT
> I hope since you're still out you're getting laid! Bow chicka wow wow 😏

I roll my eyes at her antics. She is a damn fool. The messages from my guys all read about the same, and are easy enough to respond to each quickly.

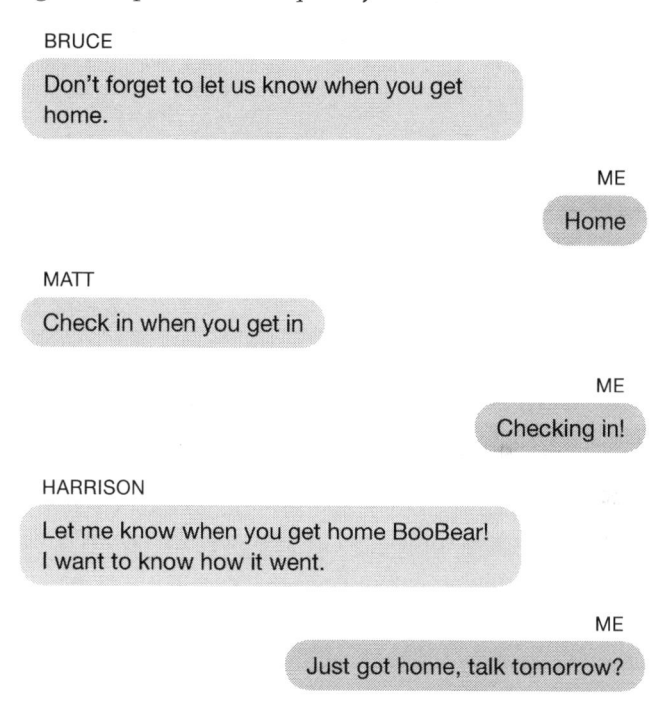

BRUCE
> Don't forget to let us know when you get home.

ME
> Home

MATT
> Check in when you get in

ME
> Checking in!

HARRISON
> Let me know when you get home BooBear! I want to know how it went.

ME
> Just got home, talk tomorrow?

Before I can open Luther's message, there's a knock on my window. It startles me enough I jump, dropping my phone in the process. "Let's go bitch you promised me food." Says Kat standing right next to my window. Picking up my phone, I open the door and glare at her. "Rude, I should keep it all for myself just for that." She sticks her tongue out at me, "You wouldn't do that, you love me too much."

Rolling my eyes because I know she's right, I tell her, "Grab those two bags from the back passenger side. I'll grab the one behind me and my stuff." She opens the back door and gasps. "What the hell did you do, Rose? Rob the restaurant?" I send a 'what the hell' look at her over the car. "No, you dork. I was Italian grandma'd." She looks thoroughly confused, "Just take them inside. I'll explain everything after I get this bra off."

Finally inside, we set the bags on the counter and I rush to the bathroom. "Don't think hiding in there will protect you, young lady! I have questions and you will give me answers!" Kat calls out. "I wouldn't dare!" I yell back. Feeling a ton better, I head back to our kitchen. Kat has pulled all the containers out of the bags and our counters are covered. She turns and looks at me, mouth hanging wide open. Looking around at all of the containers, I'm even surprised at the amount of food that was packed in those bags. "Explain, because right now, I only have two explanations in my head. Either you just spent an entire paycheck on food. Or you've become a pasta hooker selling yourself for noods."

Putting a finger up, I grab my phone and take a picture of the sheer amount of food. Opening my messages with Luther.

LUTHER

Careful Little Minx. I take being Daddy very seriously.

Remember to let me know when you're home.

ME

Do you not what to be my Daddy?

> I'm home btw. Also, I didn't comprehend just how much food Nonna sent home! LOOK AT THIS!

    I send the photo and set the phone down. Kat is looking at me expectantly. "Sorry, sorry. I had to let Luther know I was home." With that we start putting up the food, while I tell her all about my date and meeting Nonna.

    Thirty minutes and both an extremely full fridge and freezer later, we are sitting on the couch talking. She takes a huge bite of her fettuccine, while I try to contain myself at the taste of the Tiramisu in front of me. Swallowing, she points at me with her fork, "So you're telling me, that not only is this man probably one of the sweetest men either of us has ever met; but you met his grandmother on your first date?" I suck my teeth, "Yeah, I would say at a very high level that's right."

    She takes another bite, and I can tell it's to give her more time to think. "But she's not his grandmother by blood?"

    "Right, but she's his Nonna through and through".

    "And she liked you?"

    I give her an incredulous look, "Apparently so. At least that's what I'm getting from her whispering in my ear 'I like you' and then proceeding to send me home with a year's worth of food.. She even sent desserts, Kat! Desserts!"

    "You're right! She must love you to make sure you were properly sweetened up." We break out into a fit of giggles.

    "She did mention one other thing…" I trail off

    "Don't leave me hanging! What did she say!" Kats

bouncing so hard I'm sure she'll bounce herself right off this couch.

"She mentioned he had talked about me at their Sunday dinner."

"EEEEKKKK" Kat squeals, "OH MY GODDESS GIRL!!! THAT'S HUGE!!!"

"I mean, it could be.."

"Why do you sound so unsure of this whole thing?"

"Well, to start he's forty two and I'm twenty six."

"So?"

"Sixteen years is a HUGE age gap Kat. What if he decides it makes him uncomfortable?"

"Then talk to him about it? Duh!"

"We did already and he said it doesn't bother him. Well, he said it in a much smoother way than that but yeah."

"So if he already told you it doesn't bother him, what is really bothering you, girly?"

Sighing, I play with my spoon in my empty bowl. Kat sets her plate on the table before taking mine.

"Talk to me babes, is it the cunt-a-saurus?" She asks, using her oh so loving nickname for my mother.

"Or is this about Thunder-twat Emily?" Yeah, Kat's great at nicknames...

"What if they were right? What if after a while he gets tired of being seen with the fat girl on his arm? What if he realizes I'm not good enough? He is gorgeous! He could literally have anyone he wants. Why would he want to be with me?"

"Babes, you're gorgeous! As for your weight, I thought you let that go once you accepted you did nothing wrong.

You eat healthy ninety percent of the time, you're active as hell, and your size hasn't fluctuated at all in the last eight years. As for why he would want you, well I can list a few. You're absolutely beautiful, incredibly smart, funny, and have tits that double as mattresses. Wait till he experiences a titty pillow nap. He'll never be the same! Thunder-twat was an idiot and deserves the clap she gets."

"She's pushing again," I whisper.

"Who? Cunt-a-saurus?" she asks.

Nodding, I tell her about the message she sent about my 'birthday present' and all the 'don't ignore me' messages.

"Shit, that reminds me," I get up and take our dishes to the sink, grabbing my phone on my way back. "I have new messages from her." Kat groans on her side of the couch. As soon as I unlock my phone however, it's not messages from my mother I see, but new ones from Luther.

> **LUTHER**
>
> Oh there is nothing I would love more than to be your Daddy. We just need to have a conversation first.
>
> As for the food...Well, I'm not surprised by that in the slightest. I got sent home with a small bag and I still have enough food for a week. It's all going in the freezer, but it's here.
>
> I had a great time with you tonight Darlin'. I'm gonna get ready for bed. Goodnight my beautiful Little Minx.

I can't leave him on read, so before I switch threads I respond.

> **ME**
> Goodnight Luther. Thank you for a wonderful evening. Talk to you tomorrow!

"I know damn well that smile is not from your mother. What did he say?"

I turn the phone around so she can read our conversations from this evening. When she finishes reading them she looks at me like I have two heads.

"You called him Daddy! You didn't tell me that!" She squeaks more than says.

"I did, it felt...I don't know. Really good"

"EEEEPPPP!!!! When are you seeing him again?"

"I'm not sure. He leaves tomorrow on business for like two weeks."

"Well that sucks, but hey, gives y'all more time to get to know each other," she says shrugging her shoulders.

"Yeah, that's what he said, too."

"Get to know him babes. Take the chance."

"I am. Just scares me."

"Speaking of creatures of nightmares, what did cunt-a-saurus say?"

Groaning, I open our message thread.

> **BIRTH GIVER**
> You never called me Rose Marie. I think it might be best for you to move home. I have the perfect man for you, but for us to keep him we need to get you into shape quickly.
>
> He's from a good family, decently handsome, and is ready to start a family soon. Call me so we can make arrangements.

Kat snatches my phone from my hand and glares at it. Bringing her eyes back to mine, she snaps. "Is this bitch mentally insane? No way in fuck are you moving back there! Shit, you haven't even so much as visited in the last seven years and she wants you to move back? Fuck that hard...up the ass...with a sand paper dildo!"

"You're right, I'm not moving back there. I'm also in no way interested in someone she picked as acceptable for me." Taking my phone back from Kat, I text my mother back.

> ME
> Mother I'm not moving home and I'm not interested in meeting this guy. I'm living my own life and I don't need you trying to manage it.

The time catches my eye, it's almost one in the morning. Tomorrow is gonna suck. "I need to go crash, you coming?"

"Yeah, you go ahead. I'll be there in a few."

CHAPTER 23

LUTHER

I wake Friday morning with a smile on my face. Normally, my sleep is fretful when I'm traveling, but with my dreams focused on a certain beautiful brunette, I wake up feeling refreshed. Adolfo, Jamie, Nyla and I arrived in Mexico late yesterday evening, not getting to our hotel until almost eleven. After getting everyone checked in and settled, I wasted no time getting to my room and into bed. I hate that I had to leave when I did, but work doesn't stop just because I'm dating someone.

The clock on the side table reads six twelve in the morning. Our first meeting isn't until ten, giving me time to get a workout and breakfast in before we need to leave. Heading towards the bathroom to get myself together I groan. That is one downside to dreaming of my Little Minx all night, my dick is hard as granite and I have to piss. Standing at the toilet, I point the offending appendage hoping that my aim doesn't put off the hotel staff. *Waterfalls, thunderstorms, running water...shit dude come on work with me, it should not be this hard just to piss!* Finally, my body releases and I get lucky and hit my mark. It's not until I've washed my hands and am brushing my teeth, though, that my man decides to calm down.

Throwing on a pair of black basketball shorts and a work out tank, I head to the suite's living room to grab my phone off the desk. Unlocking it brings a smile to my face. We're an hour behind Austin here in Jalisco, so Rose has been up for a while. Sitting to put on my shoes I open her messages.

> **ROSE**
> Morning handsome! I hope you slept okay after traveling yesterday. I know I always struggle sleeping in a new place.
>
> Hope I'm not risking waking you up or bugging you. Just wanted to let you know I'm headed to work. TTYL!

She is so fucking adorable, but I don't want her to ever think she's bugging me. Finishing putting on my shoes, I text her back, as I head to the hotel's gym.

> **ME**
> Good morning beautiful. You didn't wake me up and you're never a bother. I slept better than expected. How did you sleep?

The gym is pretty empty this morning, which works out well for me. Putting my earbuds in, I put on my favorite work out playlist and get to work.

An hour later, I'm walking on the treadmill to cool down when my earbud is popped out of my ear. Startled, I flinch, making me miss a step. Pulling the emergency stop cord, so I don't bust my ass, I whirl to see who the hell is trying to kill me. Exclaiming, "What in the actual hell?" I watch as Jamie's smile melts, taking her from excited to scared in a flash. "I-I'm sorry L! I didn't mean to scare you, I just couldn't get your attention. I've been standing here for the last five minutes."

I had been in my own world, focusing on cooling my body down instead of my surroundings. This was way more my fault than hers. Giving her the calmest smile I can, "No Jams, that was my bad. I was unaware of my surroundings, which is exactly what I tell y'all not to do. I'm sorry for yelling and scaring you."

Pulling her to me, I hug her tight before releasing her. "It's okay L," I step away from her and grab my towel off the front of the treadmill. Turning back to her I ask, "So what brought you down here to give me heart palpitations?" The look on her face is comical as she remembers she came down here with a purpose. "Oh yeah! None of us could get ahold of you and Nyla said you probably had your phone on do not disturb. The distiller called and said he needed to push our tour back to ten forty five," she says.

"Alright, that's not a problem. Let me head up and shower. Let's meet in the restaurant at nine? That way we'll have an hour or so to eat before we head out." She beams at me. "Can do! Hey and thank you, L," she goes to turn around, but I reach out to stop her. "What are you thanking me for, Jams?" She looks shy when she answers. "For hiring my dad, and getting me the job with Nyla." I poke her nose, "You guys are family. I will never not make sure y'all are taken care of. Plus, it works out for all of us, couldn't turn down all that knowledge between the two of you," I grin at her before ushering her out of the gym.

I take my phone out of dnd mode on the way to the elevator, and it immediately starts dinging. Six missed calls, one from Nyla, one from Adolfo, two from Jamie, and two from business associates with voicemails. Choosing to deal with those later I open my messages. Jamie sent me five messages, because of course she did, and Rose replied. Opening Jamie's first, I break out into a laugh.

JAMIE

> OOOOHHH L!! Where are you?
>
> L you can't hide from me.
>
> I don't appreciate you ignoring me.
>
> Why don't you love me anymore?
>
> Fine...I'm not making you muffins anymore!

I scoff at the woman in question, "Jams, if you take away my muffins, you are going to be in so much trouble. Also, how dare you say I don't love you anymore! You're my lil princess and you know it." She beams at me, her voice is still full of sass though when she responds, "Fine, your muffin privileges won't be taken away this time. Do it again, though, and the blueberries are on the chopping block." Raising my hand in surrender, I give her what she wants, "Okay, okay. I wouldn't dare risk the blueberries." Going back to my phone, I open my messages with Rose.

> **ROSE**
> I slept okay. Kat had another nightmare last night, but I was able to pull her out of it. Took me longer to fall back asleep than it did her though. What are you up to?

> **ME**
> Just got done at the gym. Headed back to my room to shower now before meeting Adolfo and the ladies for breakfast. What about you?

The elevator stops on Jamies floor and she moves to get off. As she walks away, she says, "I'll see you in a bit. And whoever has that shit eating grin on your face...keep 'em." I don't even correct her on her language, I'm so stunned she could tell I was talking to someone I like. My phone buzzes in my hand as the elevator starts moving again.

> **ROSE**
> Who's Adolfo? And ladies?

> **ME**
> Adolfo is an old friend and my new Head of Distillery Management. As for the women traveling with us, Nyla is our Head of Marketing and Jamie is her new assistant. She also happens to be Adolfo's daughter.

> **ROSE**
> Oh, well that's cool.

> **ME**
> You never told me what you were doing.

> **ROSE**
> I'm using my FBI skills to stalk people so our teams can track them down.

What in the actual fuck.. The girl works for a rideshare company. What the hell is she doing stalking people? Back in my room, I turn on the shower and ask her just that.

> **ME**
> Why are you stalking people? I thought you said you worked for a car company?

> **ROSE**
> 😉 I do! I work for the rental team though.

> **ME**
> Still doesn't explain the stalking. Darlin' should I be worried?

She doesn't respond immediately, so I go ahead and take a quick shower. By the time I get out she's responded. I don't think I've ever dried off that fast.

> **ROSE**
> No absolutely not, unless you need to be 😉
>
> So since we rent out our cars, they all have trackers. When people don't pay their fee we tell them to bring the car back. Some people ignore those alerts, so they get sent out for repo.
>
> Unfortunately sometimes those trackers either fail or are disabled by the drivers. When that happens the repo teams can't locate them, that's where I come in.

> I created a process where I use social media to figure out where else to check. I compile a list and sent it out to our teams. People post more info than they think they do.

> I started doing it just for our office about a year ago. Now I handle all our Texas locations while also training people in other states on how to do it and what to look for. It's not an infallible method, but I currently have an 80% success rate.

ME

> That is both hot and quite terrifying. Do you enjoy it?

ROSE

> I love the hunting and tracking part of it. I hate dealing with most of our repo teams.

ME

> Why's that?

ROSE

> Because…I'm just a girl 😌 Aren't you supposed to be taking a shower?

ME

> I just got out

ROSE

> Such a tease

CHAPTER 24

LUTHER

The next few days follow the same pattern. Up with the sun, gym, breakfast, then one tour or another of different distilleries or the farms their ingredients are grown on. Through it all, Rose and I are talking day and night.

Where it would normally take months to find out this much about a partner, with our constant game of twenty questions, I feel like I know more about her than most people.

It's Thursday afternoon and our last day in Mexico. We have seen six different locations total, but only one stuck out to me so we went back today to negotiate and set up contracts. Everything is done and I honestly couldn't be happier about it. Adolfo told me the other night that even though he was devastated he lost his business the way he did, he was also relieved to not have to be the boss anymore. It was the first time I had ever really thought about stepping away from full time leadership. Running two businesses can be exhausting at times, and the more I get to know Rose, the more I think about what my future could look like outside of work.

    She's young in age, true, but she's older in mind. Talking to her and learning about the things she has experienced proves just how fast she had to grow up. Her mom never really cared what she was doing as long as she fit the mold she built for her and her dad was too busy running around having affairs and putting work first, he never cared what was going on.

    Last night, she told me her mother had pulled the funding for her schooling right before her Junior year because she declared as an English major instead of something her mother deemed 'acceptable'. She had gotten lucky with the scholarships and grants she had already received because they covered ninety percent of her tuition. She had to work full time to cover the rest of tuition, housing, and food, but she said it just taught her to appreciate what she had even more.

    How someone can be raised with such toxicity and still rise above is amazing to me. She's smart, creative, tenacious, and it just makes me want her even more. I think she is starting to trust me more, too. She's been sassy with me more and more, and hinting that she wants to have the 'rules' talk. I just don't want to do it over text. I'm sitting in the back seat of our transport with Jamie, headed back to the hotel, lost in my thoughts.

    A few minutes in, I feel a poke in my side. Turning my head, I see Jamie smiling at me. "Okay, boss man L, spill," she whisper-yells at me. "Spill what, Jams?" I ask. She rolls her eyes at me. "You have been walking around all week with stars in your eyes. I'm actually a bit offended that you haven't told me what's going on, but I'm trying to chalk it up to work trip stress. Not anymore, now spill!" Giving her a fake groan, I roll my neck around before looking at her fully, with a smile on my face. "Her name is Rose," with that, I spend the next twenty minutes of our drive telling Jamie all about the woman who is quickly taking over my mind.

We are almost back to the hotel and Jamie looks like she is about ready to jump out of her seat. "Sooooo, when are you going to claim her officially?" I pull my lips in with my teeth, I take a moment to think before answering. "I would love to do it now, but we aren't even in the same country. Having the 'rules and boundaries' conversation over text isn't really the sexiest."

Jamie rolls her eyes at me so hard I think they are going to pop out of her skull. "I know you didn't have cell phones or any way to contact each other, other than letters, and phone sex wasn't a big thing yet 'cause like you're old, but like, you can do a whole lot better than that now. There's video calls now and everything!"

My brows fly up at her bratty comment, "Have you been bodysnatched? You must have been because the Little girl I know is sweeter than my mama's sweet tea, not this sour patch kid sitting in front of me." She bursts out laughing and I stop myself from joining her. Gasping, she shoots back, "Hey, at least I'm still sweet on the inside!" I reach to tickle the little twirp, but the car comes to a stop in front of the hotel. Jamie is out of the car as soon as it stops and is skipping inside before I can even get my seatbelt off. Once I'm out of the car, Adolfo and Nyla come to stand next to me. I'm still laughing and they are both looking at me confused. "What did she do?" asks Nyla.

I'm trying to get myself together but I'm still stunned. Adolfo's attention has switched over to his daughter, and his face now looks more indulgent than anything. "Whatever it was, it must have been good to have you laughing like a crazy person and have her skipping across the lobby," Adolfo says, making Nyla chuckle.

"Let's be honest, Aldo, she would be skipping around either way." I look from them to the girl now dancing in front of the elevators. "The little turd sassed the hell out of me." Both of their eyes fly to me, "Jamie did? Sweet, compliant, doesn't even really sass me, and I'm her father, Jamie?" Adolfo looks like his head might explode at the shock of it.

"One and the same! Don't get me wrong, she was right on what she said, but she did it by calling me old." Nyla giggles, "What, did you ask her how to do something on your phone or something? Because I did the other day with a spreadsheet and she told me she was going to sign me up for a technology for geriatrics class." It's my turn to be shocked at that admission. "Well damn, she really is turning into a sour patch." Adolfo adjusts his bag on his shoulder and nods to us both. "Yup, I'm going to have a talk with miss sassy pants. Let me know what time y'all want to meet for dinner." With that he walks away.

"Really, I think she just needs a good spanking, but I'm not going to be the one to tell him that," Nyla says as we watch him leave. Turning back to me she gives me a small smile and asks, "Grab a drink with me?" I nod and wave at her to lead the way.

BREATHE

We grab a high top table in the bar and place our orders before Nyla excuses herself for a moment. Seeing her bathroom break as an opportunity to check my phone and not be rude, I see that Rose responded to my earlier message.

ME

I'm sorry Kate's still giving you flack about leaving early twice a week. It isn't her place and I still think both you and Matt should bring it up to her manager, or even HR at this point.

She isn't your manager and doing it behind his back is extremely disrespectful.

So I know you have therapy today but what other plans do you have?

ROSE

I'm headed to therapy, then I need to stop by the store. We are almost out of coffee and I ran out of my creamer this morning. Thank heavens the guys keep our secret fridge stocked for me at the office.

ME

Uh oh…Can't have you running out of coffee. That would be a danger to you and everyone else.

ROSE

Oh you have no idea. What are you doing?

ME

We just got back to the hotel. Grabbing a drink with Nyla before I head upstairs to pack.

> Jams got sassy with me today. Are you rubbing off on her telepathically?

ROSE

> Drinks with Nyla huh?

ME

> Yeah, we have some business to chat about. This way we can focus on celebrating the new contract at dinner tonight instead of borning Adolfo with marketing stuff.

ROSE

> That makes sense I guess.
>
> Also, is sass transferable telepathically? I'm pretty sure it's not. Plus, I've hung out with Jamie at the club. She is plenty sassy all on her own. Not our fault that y'all didn't know that 💅

ME

> Careful with that sass Darlin'.

ROSE

> I am very careful with my sass. Thank you very much.

ME

> Darlin' we may not have had our talk yet, but that doesn't mean I can't keep track of your sass until we do. Are you hoping to write a check your ass will have to cash 😐?

ROSE

> 😐 What are you gonna do about it? You're out of the country.

> **ME**
> Oh I have my ways...

> **ROSE**
> Promises promises... I just got to Jas' office btw.

> **ME**
> Wait...have you been texting me while driving?

> **ROSE**
> I would never 😇

> **ME**
> Rose Marie! Texting and driving is not okay. That's a safety issue and, active dynamic or not, you are in big trouble.

> **ROSE**
> Gotta go! Time for my brain to get analyzed! TTYL 😘

> **ME**
> Cute...Have a good session and text me when you get home.

"Yeah, I thought I caught a whiff of a relationship coming off of you. Who is she?" I'm startled by the question. I had seen Nyla walking back, but wasn't expecting her to read me that easily. *How do these women do that?* "I'm that transparent am I?" She looks at me like I'm insane. "Luther, I have been in your life for ten years and I've been married to your brother for seven of those, so yeah, to me you're 'that transparent'". She uses air quotes and rolls her eyes with that last bit. "Is it just sass Luther day, or is it a full moon?" I ask. "Seems like all the submissives in my life are on a roll today."

That reminds me...grabbing my phone off the table, I hold up a finger to Nyla. "Sorry, you reminded me I needed to handle something real quick." Groaning Nyla says, "I swear Luther, you better not be tattling on me to your brother. I didn't do anything wrong." I look up and she has her lip stuck out in an adorable pout. With a roll of my eyes, I ease her fears. "As much as that's a novel idea, no, I'm not texting Xai." Finding the message thread I'm looking for I send a quick text.

> **ME**
> Give me a call when you get off tonight.

I move to set my phone back down, but it vibrates almost immediately.

> **HARRISON**
> I'm about to get on a video call with one of my foremen. Do you need me to push it back and call now?

> **ME**
> Hmm...I'm pretty sure I said when you get off. It's nothing that has to be handled right now. Just need you to handle something 😈

Setting my phone back down, I turn my full attention back to Nyla. For the second time today, I gush about Rose. I'm more transparent with Nyla about the dynamic though. While I trust Jamie and she is adorable, she's still new to the lifestyle and has never had a full time dominant. Whereas Nyla has been a submissive for over a decade.

When I'm done, she reaches over and pushes my shoulder. "I wish you would have told me sooner! Hell, I can't believe it hasn't made it all over the family yet, especially with her having met Nonna of all people!" She sounds put out, like I've offended her by keeping my personal life personal. "You're right, Nonna is the gossip queen, but I think she really likes her. Actually no, I know she does. The woman sent her home with three giant bags of food that night." Nyla looks like I just told her that her husband said she didn't have to drink any water for the day. Hint: that would never happen.

"Well, this is serious then." She takes a sip of her drink looking contemplative. "Okay, hear me out. While I agree with Jamie that the ability to video call is a beautiful thing. I do think you need to have the dynamic conversation in person." I nod at her, "I agree. Just sucks because I won't see her again until next weekend." It's like my words make a lightbulb go off for Nyla. Her eyes light up, and she has a mischievous grin on her face.

"What?" I ask, slightly scared to hear what she is about to say. "Well, what if you go see her? We fly into Houston in the morning. We do have that meeting to tour the new import warehouse in Galveston at two, but that should only take a few hours. I'm sure if we call, we can adjust our flights, or at least yours. Instead of flying out of Houston Monday afternoon, we fly out of Austin. That way we could all be home for a few nights, and you can have your conversation with Rose." I look at her dumbfounded. "You just came up with that?" She shrugs, "What can I say? I'm a Genius." I smile, "That you are."

An hour later, I'm in my room packing up when I get a text from Nyla.

> **NYLA**
> We're all set! Flights changed and booked. Aldo said he'll be glad to have his own bed 😈

> **ME**
> I don't care what my brother says. You are absolutely the best.

> **NYLA**
> 🙄 That's not nice. See if I don't tell Nonna on you on Sunday!

I don't get the chance to text her back. My phone rings, Harrison's name flashing on the screen. Stealing my spine, I answer. "Good evening, Harrison." My voice comes out deeper than I expected it to, but I roll with it.

"Evening, how are you, big man?" he asks.

"I'm good, man, down in Mexico. How are you?"

He sighs, "Been busy as fuck this week, shit just keeps happening." *Well, that's no good.* "Anything I can help you with?" He chuckles dismissively, "Nah man, not unless you can make the foreman handling my Marietta project get his shit together. It's whatever, I'm just tense and stressed. Could use a release." *Hmmm..* "Well, I'll be in Atlanta next week, I could swing by and check out the site for you." He scoffs, "Nah man, I couldn't ask you to do that."

"You didn't ask me Harrison, I offered. There's a difference." Taking a deep breath, I use the opportunity to bring up what I originally called him for. "As for, release," he sucks in a breath at my words. *Interesting...* "We seem to have a naughty sub on our hands and I was hoping you could go perform some corrective action." There's a pause before Harrison responds. "What did the brat do now?" I send him a screenshot of the conversation we had earlier. "Look at the message I just sent you."

He takes a minute to read it. When he's done, his voice is dark. "So, am I just beating that ass for the safety issue or do you want a few added for her sassy ass mouth?" I moan deep in my chest, and my cock hardens to steel. Just the thought of him turning her ass a pretty shade of red again, is enough to make me leak in my boxers. "Just the safety issue this time. I won't lie though, I would love to watch." It's his turn to moan. "I'll head that way in a bit. I'll see what I can do."

"You do that," and right before I disconnect, I add in a low tone, "and I'll see what else I can do to help you relieve that tension."

CHAPTER 25

ROSE

I'm standing in the kitchen zoning out while dinner heats up. We are still eating leftovers from Luther's Nonna and it's been a week. I'm glad she sent home a variety of things or I would seriously be in danger of starting to dislike my favorite foods. Kat's out with some of her old coworkers at a concert, so I'm not expecting her home anytime soon, if she comes home tonight at all. So, I'm excited to enjoy some quiet time.

I'm curled up on the couch reading while I eat, when my phone goes off. The message that pops up squashes my plans of a quiet night researching through smut, with a quickness.

HARRISON
I will be there in fifteen minutes. We need to have a serious conversation, Sweetheart.

Shit, he called me Sweetheart instead of BooBear. That means Harrison is in Sir mode, not best friend mode. That also reminds me...I need to talk to him about where we go from here. Texting him back, I try to find out what's up.

ME
What do we need to talk about? And why do I feel like I'm in trouble?

I sit there and stare at my phone for a few minutes. My appetite gone, I go through my week. Trying to figure out what I could possibly be in trouble for. It isn't often that Harrison flips to Sir outside of a scene, but when he does there is always a reason. I can't come up with anything, but as I walk into the kitchen to clean my plate it hits me. Setting my plate down on the counter, I rush back to the couch, grab my phone and text Luther.

ME
You didn't!!

LUTHER
I didn't what Minx?

ME
Did you tell on me to Harrison?

LUTHER
Hmm...I wouldn't say I told on you, but I did ask a mutual friend of ours to handle some business for me.

Since, as you pointed out earlier, I'm out of the country and can't handle it myself.

The knock on my door, mixed with Luther's response, has my heart racing. I know once I let Harrison in, my ass is grass. *Dammit, and I have dealership runs to do tomorrow.* Walking over to the door, I do my now normal checks to make sure it's actually Harrison and then open the door. Not even greeting him before I wave him in. I've barely turned the lock before, I feel him standing behind me, causing my body to freeze and my breath to hitch. His hand takes hold of my ponytail, using it to pull my head backwards. "Safeword?" He asks. "Pothos," I respond quickly. That's all I get out before I'm led back into the living room.

"Kneel," he growls at me. *Shit, he is really pissed.* I don't hesitate, kneeling on the floor next to the arm of my couch. "Look at me," his voice is hard and demanding. "Have you figured out that you are in fact in trouble, Rose? You have permission to speak." I clear my throat, trying to center myself before I respond. "Yes, Sir," my voice is smaller than normal. "And you understand you are not just in trouble with me, correct?" I damn sure know I am, "Yes, Sir."

He nods at me, before setting his backpack on the table. "Sweetheart, because this is the first time you have gotten in trouble with multiple people we are going to have a conversation regarding consent, prior to having the corrective conversation."

"Yes, Sir, what would you like to discuss?" I ask him. "The first thing I would like to know is your current color." I give him a small smile, "Overall, I'm green, Sir." He lowers himself on the couch bringing our eye level closer, "Good, second I need to ask you, do I still have your consent to handle your punishment? I know you are seeing Luther now, and I do not want to overstep with you."

Just him asking that makes my heart swell for my best

friend. We haven't discussed the shift in our dynamic yet, even though we both know it's shifting. It's not that we don't want to acknowledge the shift, but Luther and I haven't discussed it, so I wouldn't know what to tell him. "Yes, Sir, I trust you and I know I broke a major rule. You still very much have my consent."

It's true, Harrison is usually really laid back in our dynamic. Since he isn't my full time dom, it's usually funishments we deal with and those are all during a scene session. There have been a few times where I've asked for a maintenance spanking, when I've been really stressed or overwhelmed, but those weren't sexual. There have only been three other times I've actually been in trouble with Harrison, and they were all health or safety related. Those rules are big deals to any Dom, but with Harrison they are major.

"Thank you for that, Sweetheart. Last, I need to ask for your consent for Luther to join us via video call. He has requested that he be present for your punishment." A giggle escapes me, "Of course, he did," I say. "Can you blame him? But if you don't want him to join us, I can always tell him no. He will understand." I shake my head at him, "Sir, may I ask you a question before I answer?" He gives me a sharp nod, "Of course, Sweetheart."

"Are you okay with him joining?" His smile is small, but sincere. "Yes, Sweetheart, I am. When it comes to this I fully believe he has every right to be involved. I may still be a bit conflicted with how he makes me feel, but that has nothing to do with this." He reaches out and squeezes my shoulder, "So, what is your decision?" There is only one answer, "I consent, you can call him."

Harrison sets up his laptop on the table, it's angled perfectly to get us both in the frame. While he's setting up, my mind wanders to the fact I'm glad I chose decent comfy clothes tonight and I don't look like a complete slouch. I'm not wearing any makeup but it is what it is. Not like we haven't shared photos this weekend. Only difference is there's not going to be any filters to hide my blemishes or scars. He is going to have to accept all of them if he truly wants this, wants me.

My attention is brought back to the present when I hear the call ringing on the computer. It only rings twice before Luther answers, "Hey, Harrison, give me just a second. I just got off the elevator and I'm almost to my room." I can hear his movements through the speakers, but I know better than to look up. "No problem, are you alone?" Harrison asks. "Absolutely, I would never put our business out like that."

I hear a beep and assume it's the door to his room. The sound of the handle turning in the next second confirms it for me. "Our business, huh?" Harrison chuckles out. "Very much so, Harrison. As far as I'm concerned, when it comes to Rose, we are a team. For now at least, but that's a conversation for another time."

I hear more shuffling, *what is he doing?* I get my answer a moment later when a ding goes off signaling someone else joined the call followed immediately by another sound signaling a disconnect. "Alright, now that I'm on my computer, where are we?" Luther's voice is harder than I've ever heard it before.

"We've only discussed headspace and consent, I was waiting to continue until you were with us." I hear a hum before Luther says my name, "Rose, look at me please." Raising my head I face the computer screen. "Good girl, now I know you've already shared your color with Harrison, but can you please tell me?" Meekly, I respond, "Umm, yes, I'm uh green."

He shifts his head to the side. Looking at me with apprehension. "Darlin', you don't sound sure. What's wrong?" *Shit, he heard my blunder.* "Nothings wrong, per se," I tell him. "I'm just not sure how to address you at the moment." Nodding toward Harrison, I continue, "I know to address him as Sir, but what should I call you?" Luther smirks before asking, "What would you like to address me as, this evening, Minx?"

I use my nails to scratch at the skin on my knees while I bite my lip. Harrison reaches down, setting his hands over mine to stop me. When he squeezes them I meet his eyes, "Just be honest with him and tell him what you want. I've got you." He whispers before releasing me.

Returning my attention to Luther, I say "Daddy," my voice is quiet, too quiet if I'm honest, so I close my eyes briefly while taking a deep breath. When my eyes meet his again through the screen, my voice is louder and more confident. "Daddy, I want to call you Daddy."

The smile that takes over his face is down right x-rated and causes a chill to run through me. When he speaks his tone is dark and hungry, "Daddy it is, Minx. Now do you need me to revisit the consent conversation, or would you like to move forward with your punishment?" The feeling of both their eyes on me is heavy. Steeling myself for what is to come, I give my answer. "We can move ahead. I have already given consent and I trust you, both." My words seem to cause a physical reaction in Luther, but he pushes forward. I watch him adjust and lean in towards the computer. "That pleases me to hear. Now, let's address why we are in this current situation. Tell me, Rose. Why are you in trouble this evening?"

Adjusting my position slightly, I answer, "I was texting Daddy while driving. As well as sassing Daddy." Luther shakes his head, slightly. "That's partially correct, Rose. So, I'll correct you. You are not in trouble for the sassing. In this situation, you are only in trouble for texting while driving. Can you tell me why you decided to make that choice, Rose?"

I bite my lip and lower my head, "Because I wanted to keep talking to you, but didn't want to bother you with a phone call." Bringing my eyes back to his, I manage to catch the flare of what I think is disappointment? He didn't seem angry really, but I can tell he doesn't like my answer.

"What did I tell you about your ability to contact me?" He asks. "You told me that I could text or call you whenever I want, and that if you weren't able to talk you would let me know." He nods at my answer. "Exactly, Rose, and had you called you would have known I was perfectly in a position to talk to you. I know we are still new to this relationship, but just know, I will always make you my top priority."

Grabbing my chin, Harrison forces my eyes to him, "Now tell me, Rose, what rules do almost all dominants require their submissive to follow?" Harrison's tone is hoarse as he asks. Quietly I say, "Health and safety rules, Sir." His eyes darken further showing me just how upset he is with this situation.

From the computer, Luther addresses me, but Harrison

doesn't allow me to look at him. "I love that you didn't want to stop talking to me, but I will never be okay with you compromising your safety to do it. When you revealed that you had been texting me while driving, everything that could have happened ran through my mind and it terrified me. I just found you, Darlin', and I don't want to lose you because you weren't being safe. So, with safety being a universal rule in general, as well as something you have previously agreed on with Harrison, he is going to take over from here." I use what little room I have in Harrison's grip to give Luther a small nod. "I understand, Daddy."

"Sweetheart, there are very few things that would get you severely punished by me and you know it. You broke my number one rule. This is going to be hard and fast. For every text you sent while driving you will receive five swats with my palm and a lash from my belt. Do you understand and accept?" A shiver of dismay shoots down my spine, but I say "Yes" anyways. *This is going to suck.* Harrison addresses Luther next, "Luther, do me a solid while I get her in position. Check your thread with Rose and tell me how many messages she sent while driving today."

Harrison helps me stand and leads me to the arm of the couch. "Strip" he demands. I take my clothes off without protest, knowing that arguing would only make this worse for me. "Now, bend over the arm of the couch, arms stretched out in front of you." Again, I do as instructed. Harrison adjusts the angle of the computer slightly, making sure that Luther has a prime view for the show he's about to make of my ass. As soon as he is finished he asks Luther, "Do you have a number for me?" Luther's face is telling and I know it's going to be even worse than I thought, as he says his next words. "Looks like the number is six."

My mind rushes to try and do the math, but Harrison is faster. "Thirty with my hand and six with the belt," he says as he removes his belt from its resting place on his hips. "Hang on tight Sweetheart, this is gonna hurt."

I'm damn positive my ass is going to fall off, as he lands his final blow with his belt. I faintly hear his belt hit the floor behind me, but it's hard to focus on anything with the way I'm currently crying. Harrison gently picks me up and sits back on the couch with me in his lap. I have never been more grateful for man spread in my life, as my now screaming behind rests between his legs. It takes me more than a few minutes to calm my breathing enough to focus on my surroundings. As my mind becomes clearer, I start to hear both Harrison and Luther speaking calming words to me.

"Good Girl, Sweetheart."

"That's it, Darlin', in through your nose, out through your mouth."

"Sweetheart, you took your punishment so well. It's all over now."

Harrison is rubbing his hand up and down my spine, centering me to where I am. When I'm finally at the point of being able to speak, I pull my face away from Harrison's neck. His shirt and neck are covered in both my tears and snot, which makes me feel even worse. "I - I'm so-oh-o s-s-sorry, I - I got-t my ick all over you!" I say between hiccuping sobs. "It's not a big deal, Sweetheart. Nothing a washer can't handle."

Harrison shifts us both, while reaching for something on the table. The movement causes my butt to rub against his jeans and I whimper at the feeling. "Shhh Darlin', I know it hurts, but you did so well." Luther soothes. When he grabs what he was reaching for, Harrison leans back enough that I can look over at Luther. "I - I'm so sorry I scared y-you today, Da-Daddy. I didn't mean to, I really di-didn't. I wa-wasn't thinking." I manage to pant out.

"I know, Darlin', I know. Hopefully next time you'll think before you do it and will remember this." He winks at me and I frown. "You, Daddy, do not seem to understand just how bad my ass hurts right now! I won't ever be texting and driving again!" He chuckles, "Alright, my Little Minx."

Harrison brings a wet towel to my face and starts to wipe it off. Caught off guard by the feeling, I reflexively shrink back. Immediately, fire shoots across my ass leaving a deep throbbing pain in its wake. I cry out from the pain, and Harrison tightens his arm around me. "It's gonna be okay, Sweetheart, I just want to clean up your face before I lay you down okay?" Another small whimper leaves me, and I can't bring myself to speak, choosing instead to nod my acceptance.

It doesn't take long for Harrison to get my face wiped down. The cool cloth feels great against my heated skin, and I'm tired enough that I don't even argue when he holds the cloth to my nose and tells me to blow. "You are being so cooperative, Sweetheart. I am so proud of you." His praise makes me feel all sorts of warm inside. "I'm going to lay you down on your front so I can put some Arnica on your backside."

He lifts me and lays me down on the couch. My head is in just the right spot that I can see Luther still on the screen.

"This may sting a little, but stay still for me okay?" I give him another lazy nod and he shifts to the other side of the couch.

Luther gives me a sweet smile, "Hey there, Darlin'." My voice is airy and light when I respond. "Hi, Daddy," his face shifts as I wince at the feel of the cool gel against what I'm sure is very bruised flesh. "Are you okay?" I ask. "I'm okay, just wish I was the one there taking care of you." That brings a smile to my face, and I try to make him feel better. "Soon, Daddy, soon. At least you know until then, I'm in good hands."

He makes an affirmative sound. "You're absolutely right. Now, why don't you close your eyes and rest for a minute. Harrison isn't leaving until you are all squared away and asleep." I feel my eyes getting heavier and I have the idea that he has the right idea. "Okay, Daddy. But just for a minute." Letting the darkness pull me off to sleep.

CHAPTER 26

LUTHER

Today has been nothing but a pure shit show. From the moment we landed in Houston, it has been one thing going wrong after another. It started with Nylas bag not making it onto our flight. Which delayed us in leaving the airport, so we could alert the airline. They were unable to give us an answer of where the bags went while we were there, and as far as I know, are still trying to figure out where exactly they went. Once we finally left the airport, we got caught behind an accident involving a five car pile up that ended with an 18-wheeler on its side blocking all but one lane. So a trip that should have taken us about an hour, ended up taking us three.

When we did finally reach the warehouse, we found that it is in need of major renovations in order to be up to code. Which will take months and more money than I had originally dedicated to the project. It isn't like we have much of a choice though, we already signed on the building. Now we are once again sitting in traffic, headed back to the Houston

Airport to fly home for the weekend. I am mentally and physically exhausted, but I am also itching to see my girl.

Nyla turns in her seat to face me and asks "So are you going over to surprise your girl tonight, or what is your plan?" Groaning, I tell her, "No, I think I am going to go home and sleep tonight. Then surprise her with the fact I'm in town in the morning." She nods, "I think that is a good idea. You have had a long and stressful day. A good night's sleep will not only help you decompress, but will help you go into y'all's conversation with a clear mind." I shoot her a wink, "My thoughts exactly."

We arrive back at the airport with only an hour to spare before our connecting flight and we are all a little worse for wear. By the time they call for boarding, I am fully grouchy and more than ready to be home in my bed. Pulling out my phone, I send Rose a text letting her know that I'm going to be disconnected for a while, just like I promised her.

I wake up the next morning feeling energetic, anticipating what today will hold. Grabbing my phone off my nightstand, I quickly realize it is only five am, on a Saturday. Yep, I'm not texting Rose this early. *I have more self-preservation than that.* Instead, I quickly change and go for a run. An hour and a half later, I'm walking into my building drenched in sweat but with my eyes set on my prize. Walking into my apartment, I text Rose.

ME

> Good Morning Darlin'. I hope you slept well. Let me know when you wake up. I want to know what you have planned today.

BREATHE

Setting my phone down on the kitchen table, I head into my bathroom and get showered for the day. I still don't have a response by the time I have showered, shaved, and got ready. But it is only seven forty-five, so I'm not too worried about it.

I brew a cup of coffee and sit at the table, pulling out my laptop to review a couple of emails. I'm reviewing a renewal contract a little while later when my phone vibrates next to me.

ROSE
Good Morning Daddy. You were up early.

ME
Yeah. I'm re-adjusting to the time difference. You didn't answer my question tho. What do you have planned for today?

ROSE
Nothing really. Kat and Harrison have plans tonight to go see a rock concert, but it's not a band I like so I'm not going.

Other than that I have a few errands to run. Including shopping with those two crazies. Then I'll just be hanging at the house. What about you?

ME
Right now I'm reviewing a renewal contract, but I was hoping I could discuss a completely different kind of contract with someone I would to make things official with.

ROSE
Ooo, do you want to schedule a video call?

ME

Well, I was thinking more along the lines of dinner at my place?

ROSE

Wait a second, I thought you were out of town.

ME

I wanted to surprise you. I got in late last night. Figured this conversation would be best in person and I have a few days between meetings.

ROSE

I'd love to! What do you want me to bring?

ME

That depends on if you are staying the night or not. If you are, you will need an outfit for tomorrow.

ROSE

What about pajamas?

ME

I've got that covered.

ROSE

I bet you do 😏. When would you want me to come over?

ME

I mean you could come over now and I wouldn't complain. I do have another question for you in regard to our discussion this evening.

> **ROSE**
> Well out with it Mister!

> **ME**
> I know it's unorthodox, but how would you feel about me pulling your limits list from the club files? I'll pull mine too just to make it easier to compare.

> **ROSE**
> I would be okay with that. As long as we open them together. That way we can both be surprised at the same time.

> **ME**
> Alright, I'll have them brought over. Let me know what time you want to come over.

> **ROSE**
> It's probably going to be closer to mid/late afternoon. Shopping with the 'Ooo Look' twins is never fast.

> **ME**
> Alright Darlin'. Just let me know when y'all are headed back to the apartment.

Smiling, I switch over my message thread with my sister Aniya.

> **ME**
> Hey baby sis. I need you to do me a favor.

> **ANIYA**
> Lucky for you I am feeling generous today. What can I do you for?

> **ME**
> I need you to pull two files and have copies sent over.

> **ANIYA**
> Uh, wth for? Isn't that a breach of privacy?
>
> Wait let me answer that for you…yes, yes it is!

> **ME**
> It's only a breach of privacy on one seeing as how one of the files you'll pull is mine. With the other one, I have her permission.

> **ANIYA**
> Oh, is this that girl I heard you're seeing?

> **ME**
> I see the family chat has been active. Yes it is. Rose Morrow

> **ANIYA**
> Give me an hour and I'll send your idiot little brother over with them.

> **ME**
> Thanks sis. You know you're my favorite sister.

> **ANIYA**
> Jackass, I'm your only sister.

It's been almost five hours now since I talked to Anyia. *One hour my ass!* There's a knock at my door, and when I open it, I see my baby brother Kylo standing there. "Well, you aren't the brother I thought I was going to be seeing today," I say to him while pulling him in for a hug. "When did you get back into town?" Slapping my back, he chuckles. "I got back the day before yesterday for a few days. Head back out Monday morning at the ass crack of dawn. What's this I hear about you finding a girl that actually likes your ass?"

I can't help the smile that crosses my face when he brings her up. "Rumors are true, her name is Rose. She is coming over later tonight to discuss our dynamic. Which is why I need these," I say plucking the files out of his hand. "Are you sure you want to invade her privacy this way, Bro?" I roll my eyes at him, "I'm not invading her privacy, Jackass. We are going through them together. I'm not even opening until she gets here."

He actually looks relieved, "Well, that makes me feel better."

"What's this I hear that she's already met Nonna?" Kylo asks. "Yeah, she has. By accident, if I'm being honest, but Nonna likes her and wants me to bring her to Sunday dinner tomorrow." Kylo looks stunned, "Have you told mom and dad?" I look at him like he's insane, "I talked to them about her yesterday and they're excited to meet her, but I haven't discussed dinner with her yet so I don't know. Are you going to be at dinner?"

It's his turn to look at me like I'm off my rocker. "Really dude. Do you think I can be in town and get away with missing Sunday dinner? Nonna would have my balls if I tried to do that." Laughing, I bring up something I've been meaning to talk to him about. "You're right, she definitely would. You know, we could hire someone to go to all these conventions. You don't have to do them all yourself." He smirks at me with a wink, "I like going. Plus who knows I may just meet the Little of my dreams while I'm out on the road." *Or you could be here long enough for me to introduce you to the Little Brat that I think would fit you.* "Well I have a meeting in an hour and a half and I would like to be at home for it, so enjoy."

There's a knock at the door as we are walking to it, "Was she supposed to be here already?" Shaking my head, I tell him, "No, she is out running errands and shopping with friends. That's the grocery delivery I ordered for tonight. I'm grilling some steaks." He helps me bring in the groceries before he heads out. "Well, don't do anything I wouldn't do, Old Man. I'll see you tomorrow night, and hopefully, get to meet the new misses."

About an hour later, I get a text from Rose. She's letting me know that they were on their way home and she is grabbing her bag and heading my way. I let her know I am excited to see her, before sending her my address and door code.

CHAPTER 27

ROSE

Walking up to Luther's door, my heart pounds erratically. This is it, the conversation I have been both anticipating and dreading in kind. Taking a deep breath, I reach up and knock on the door. I don't have to wait long for Luther to answer, it was almost as if he was waiting for me. He's standing there looking edible in snug fitting dark wash jeans and a form fitting olive colored shirt.

His voice is almost a purr when he greets me, "Good evening beautiful. Come in." Underwear ruined...instantly...

Walking into the apartment, I'm stunned by its beauty. The apartment was built with an open floor plan, with the kitchen facing the living and dining area. Decorated with dark tones, and sparsely, the space is tastefully done. You can definitely tell that a man lives here, but you can also tell it was a woman that decorated.

"Thank you for having me" I say, my voice huskier than I expected it to be. "Your home is absolutely beautiful!" His hands land on the tops of my arms, causing me to jump just a little. I hadn't expected him to be standing right behind me. Leaning in, he whispers in my ear, "It does the job, but the view just got a whole better in my opinion."

Shivers run down my spine at the tone of his voice. He runs his hands down the outsides of my arms, making the hairs stand on edge. "Mhm, I've missed you," he growls. Tilting my head backwards, I accept his kiss when he leans. The kiss is fierce, and sets my blood a boil, but still gentle, causing my toes to curl. When he pulls away, I sigh "I've missed you, too."

"Let me give you the tour, before we get distracted," he says, taking my hand to lead the way. As we pass the overstuffed navy couch, I lean over and set my purse down. Luther leads me to the hallway on the other side of the living room. There are two smaller bedrooms off the hall. Both rooms are open and decorated beautifully. The first is done with light and cozy fabrics, and almost feminine decor, with different shades of creams. The second is a mirror of the first, but in shades of misty blues that remind me of early mornings in spring. Continuing down the hall, we pass a guest bath that isn't completely decorated but is no less beautiful.

At the end of the hall is a set of double doors. He opens them to reveal a huge bed that seems to be built into the wall. The dark wood beams running from the floor to the ceiling, make it seem even larger. The bedding is all dark gray and navy, giving fuel to the masculine energy radiating from the space. It's both beautiful and intimidating. One of the walls is made of just glass. The large picturesque windows give the bedroom a beautiful city backdrop. There are blackout curtains hanging at the edges, but something tells me this man never sees the need to use them.

"Wow," I sigh, "this is spectacular." Lightly, he squeezes my hand. "Thank you, but you haven't seen my favorite parts yet," I look at him in disbelief. "It gets better?" With a knowing smirk, he leads me toward a door on the other side of the room.

What I see when the door opens and I step inside, can only be described as magical. A huge white soaker tub large enough to fit four people, sits in the corner of the room with a large rainfall shower head mounted above. The dark blue shower stall, or should I say room, to the left is, dare I say, what dreams are made of. There are so many nozzles and sprayers I wouldn't even know where to start.

His and hers bowl style sinks look to be made of crystals and take my breath away. Looking up at Luther I spit out, "You may never get me out of here, I just want you to know that." He chuckles, and looks down at me with soft eyes, "It's yours, Darlin', whenever you want it." I give him a side-eyed look, "I want you to remember that when I look like a damn plump raisin and you still can't get me out of that tub. Your words not mine, Buster."

"Come on, Little Minx. Let me show you the kitchen. I promise you can soak to your heart's content later."

The kitchen has a warm and cozy feel while still being as open as the rest of the apartment. With a chef style stove and a farmhouse sink, it's easy to see how someone could get lost cooking in here. The dark wood of the cabinetry matches the rest of the wood throughout, managing a perfect balance with the lighter counters. The entire apartment feels warm and inviting.

"This entire place is amazing! How long have you lived here?" I asked. Luther runs his hand over his chin, "I bought it about five years ago, I think. It was close to both the office and the club, so to me it was a no brainer." He says with a shrug.

Looking around, I notice that even though the space is beautifully decorated it's missing something. "For you living here for five years, it doesn't have a lot of personal touches." I point out.

"I haven't spent a lot of time here. It's just a house. Somewhere for me to lay my head at night and store my things. If it wasn't for Mom, I'm pretty sure it would look like a complete bachelor pad. I can't say I wouldn't love to see it become a home one day, though." He clears his throat, "Maybe even some day in the near future."

My body warms at his words. *Girl you are probably taking him way too seriously. Abort! Change the damn subject.* "So, tonight was all you and it looks like you have it all planned out." I smile at him, giving him my best doe eyes in the process. "So, what do you have planned for us?"

His smile is soothing, but I can see the heat hidden in his eyes when he speaks, "Well, by the time tonight is over, I want you to officially be mine. I figure since it's still early, we can start by reviewing each other's list of limits and discuss them. Afterwards, we can discuss what we both want, while I make dinner. How does that sound?"

"Sounds like a plan, Big Man." I say with a playful tone, as I move towards the couch. A growl comes from deep in his chest that I feel all throughout my body as he stalks closer to me.

"That is the second time since you walked through that door, you have called me something other than the two names you are supposed to use."

Wanting to see where he will take this, I decide to poke the bear. "Oh, you have more than one name I should be using? I was unaware. Please do enlighten me, Mr. Breedlove"

His body is flush with mine now. "That's three, Minx. To answer your question though, as of last night, there are only two names you should be calling me."

Leaning into me further, he palms the nape of my neck and brings my ear to his mouth. His tone is dark and feels like pure fire against my skin. I can't help the small moan that slips past my lips, before I ask, "And what are these names?"

He bites down on my earlobe, before he says words that damn near make my heart stop. "If we are in public or somewhere you aren't comfortable, then I have no issues with you calling me Luther." His hand tightens around me, not enough to hurt, but definitely enough to have my entire body at attention.

"Any other time, my Little Minx." He licks my ear, "My," nip, "name," nip, "is," nip, "Daddy." He punctuates his words with a final hard bite on my earlobe. Ripping a moan out of me and ending any chance my underwear had of not being ruined.

"I think I can handle that." I whisper.

"Then say it," his tone is demanding, and I almost give in.

But no matter how much I want to give him what he's craving, I want to test him more.

My voice is almost imperceptible, "I'm glad we had this conversation, Luther." I tried to move away from him, but don't make it far, as his name leaves my mouth.

His arm wraps around my waist, while the hand on my nape moves into my hair. Pulling my head back to make me look at him, he asks, "Are we in public, Little Minx?" *Ooo, Daddy looks sexy when he's grumpy.* "No." A groan comes from low in his chest "No what, Minx?"

"No, Daddy." I grind my hips against his, but he pulls back before we can go any further.

"Smart choice, Minx." He says as he turns me to face the table. "The folders on the table are both of our limits lists. Go sit down and wait for me. Would you like wine or a mixed drink?"

Answering with a frustrated huff, I tell him, "For this conversation, the good stuff." I can hear the rumble in his chest as he fights back his laugh. "Am I safe to assume by good stuff you mean tequila?"

"Yes, please, Daddy." I have only managed to take one full step before I feel his palm land against my ass. I let out a surprised squeal on contact and whirl on him with a glare. He doesn't say a word, just winks and heads to the kitchen.

I take a seat at the table, a bit confused because I am looking down at three folders. Luther walks back into the dinning area carrying two glasses. "Tequila and Sprite, Darlin'." Thanking him, I point down at the folders in front of us. "Question, is there another person we are waiting on?"

"No," he says with a chuckle. "These are the lists I had

pulled from our files at the club," he tells me, tapping the first two.

Pointing at the last one, he continues, "That one there, is a personal contract for just the two of us. I think it is important that we set our boundaries not just for at the club, but also for our relationship in full."

"I can understand that." I say with a nod. Luther hands me the folder on top, and keeps the other. Opening it, I realize that he has given me his and kept mine.

"I figured we could do this the easiest way possible. You will look over the 'Yes', 'No', and 'Maybe's on mine and I'll do the same with yours. If we have any clarifying questions, we can just ask." He shrugs and continues, "On mine most of everything is marked either 'Yes' or 'No' and the ones that are marked 'No' will probably not change."

Shyly, I smile at him, "Um, I think all of mine are 'Yes' or 'No', too. I don't care for much wiggle room on things I'm not willing to do." He smiles down at me and then we both get to reading. The room is quiet as we review the forms, but I can't stop the giggle that comes from me when I get to one of the lines. "What has you giggling?" He asks.

"Hmmm, no skat play, huh?" He looks at me like I have two heads, "Yeah, no. I also don't do the whole golden shower thing either."

I giggle at his face, "While I don't yuck on anyone's yum, and will fight with anyone who does. We can both agree on that staying out of our play time." Which makes him full belly laugh.

Pausing he looks at my list, then me, "Yours also says no fisting of any kind, is that a hard limit for you?"

Rolling my eyes, I tell him, "Yeah, it is. I'm not a cat and she's not a box. It does not fit and it will not sit." That sends him into a fit of laughter.

"Heard loud and clear," he says. Putting up his hands in a sign of surrender.

"From what I am seeing, we are pretty much on the same page about everything. I find it interesting though that you have age play as a maybe." I say, giving him a curious look.

He gives me a sheepish smile, "I was being honest when I told you that having a Little isn't my thing. The choice to add that to my willing to do list, was for club purposes. If someone I care about is there and they need a Big for the night. I would be happy to fill in, but again, it's not my thing."

My heart swells, and I smile, "I see and I can respect it."

I fidget in my seat a little, "There is one other thing I wanted to talk to you about before we finish the limits conversation. Obviously, these were meant for while inside the club. What are your views on sharing as a whole?" My question comes out in a rush, but at least it's out there.

He doesn't seem surprised by my question, "I wondered when we were going to talk about Harrison. That is who you meant, right?"

Nervously I look away, "For the most part, but what if, I don't know, say Nyla wanted to play with you while you're on a business trip or something?" *Okay, so apparently I'm still a little insecure about that...I'm not sure why I would feel okay with him playing with another man, but scared of another woman.*

Luther looks shocked by my question, "Nyla? Why would you think that would ever happen?"

I can't bring myself to look at him when I say what's been on my mind. "Well, y'all were spending a lot of time together on this last trip. I just thought, what if she wanted to do more?"

He reaches over and lifts my face with a finger under my chin. When our eyes meet, all I see is understanding, "First of all, Darlin', let me make something clear. I have not nor will I ever be attracted to Nyla."

I start to relax, but then his next words hit me like a ten pound bag of bricks. "Secondly, Nyla is my sister-in-law."

OH MY GOD! I throw my head backwards before bringing it down to the table and try to cover myself with my hands "I'm an idiot and I'm sorry." I know it had to sound like nothing more than a dramatic grumble but apparently he understood.

He moves my hands out of the way and makes me look at him again. "Don't call yourself names. You can ask me anything and I won't ever lie to you about it. Just talk to me."

Biting my lip, I tell him, "I can do that. Or at least I can try." The smile he gives me almost stops my heart.

Clearing his throat, he pushes forward. "Now that we've got that cleared up. Let's go back to your original question about sharing. Inside the club, as long as whichever of us is interested in another partner for that night, tells the other and we discuss it, I'm fine with other partners, as long as we both agree. Now, outside of the club," he places my face in his palm, "I would never try to take Harrison from you, Darlin'. Plus, it's quite convenient to be able to call in backup. As long as our relationship is respected, I am good with it."

Pulling my lips in, I run my gaze over him. Taking in just

how delectable this man really is. "I've seen the way you look at him, Daddy. He looks at you the same way." He gives me a look that says he doesn't know why I'm telling him this. "Listen, I'm not saying you have to, but what I am saying is that if you wanted to try something with him too...I am more than okay with it."

Leaving that subject alone for now, because I have a feeling he is going to need time to stew on it. I change the subject.

"Alright then, what else do you have for me?" Smiling, He slides over the other folder.

"This isn't something for us to do together right now. It is something for us to build to, though. I want you to read over it during the next few weeks and adjust anything you want or need to. Then we will revisit it in say, a month."

He places his hand back on my palm, while the other grabs my hand and squeezes.

"Rose, I want to be all in with you, but I won't let you go all in with me blind. You need to understand what it means to be mine, I will own you in every way a man can own a woman. I will consume your mind, devour your body, and claim your soul. I will take your body at every opportunity, no matter where we are. I will use you in ways you have never even imagined, leaving you breathless, sore and wanting more. I will ruin you for anyone else, and you know what?"

My heart is beating wilder than a rabbits and I know my eyes are almost out of their sockets. I shake my head no because I am unable to form any words.

"You will crave the deprived things I will do to you. You will thank me every single time and beg for more. You will not only be Daddy's fantastic and bratty Darlin', who he will spoil and treat like a queen. You'll also be Daddy's perfect little whore, whose body I will leave destroyed over and over again.

Where the hell did this man come from? I know my underwear is destroyed and I won't be surprised if I leave a huge puddle in this chair when I get up. *Fuckkk!*

"For now though, we'll go with what we'll call dynamic lite." The whiplash this just man just gave me is jarring.

"Dynamic lite?" I ask, cocking my head.

"Yes, Darlin', I need you to be ready for all that I am. Just as I need to be ready for all of you. By the time we sign that contract, we will both know who we belong to."

Stick a fork in me because, I AM FUCKING DONE!

"Until we have a signed agreement, do I have your consent to organize things like surprises, both regular and spicy, give you orders within reason, and take you within reason following the guidelines of our limits."

"YOU ARE A WALKING NEON GREEN FLAG!" I exclaim.

He gives me a devious smile, "Don't worry Minx, my flags have another side. But you'll only ever see the one covered in coal come out in other ways. I think you'll love just how dirty they are."

Licking his lips, he points out my blunder, "You never answered my question, Darlin'. Do I have your consent?"

Smiling, I nod, "Yes, Daddy. I think I would like that."

Luther

I'm in the kitchen a little while later, using my indoor grill to cook our steaks. We already made garlic mashed potatoes and Rose made some asparagus, so as soon as the steaks are done we are ready to eat.

Tonight has been full of intense conversations for both of us. Needing some air and wanting to enjoy the view, Rose stepped out onto the back patio.

I haven't been able to get what she mentioned about Harrison wanting me, too, off my mind since she brought it up earlier. She's right to think I want him. I would be stupid to deny it, at this point, but I never entertained it because I didn't think he saw men that way.

Well, today has been full of 'go for it' moments, what is one more?

Taking this as an opportunity to not only surprise her, but to maybe, just maybe, surprise him, too. Pulling my phone out from my back pocket, I decide to just jump. I open my message thread with Harrison and dive headfirst.

> ME
> What time do y'all think you will be out of the concert tonight?

It doesn't take him long to respond at all.

> HARRISON
> Kat only wants to stay for the first two acts. So I would say probably around 9. Why, what's up? Does Rose need another adjustment?

> ME
> No, but how would you feel about meeting us at the club after you're done?

> **HARRISON**
> I could do that.

> **ME**
> Wonderful. Let me know when y'all are leaving the concert and we will meet you there.

The steaks are finished, when I put my phone back in my pocket. I place everything on the table before heading to the back patio. Walking over to stand behind Rose, I slide my arms around her waist.

"Hey Darlin', are you enjoying the view? Cause I definitely am."

She giggles "It is pretty damn magnificent out here," and I can hear the smile in her voice. "Is dinner ready?"

Placing a kiss on the top of her head, "Yeah, Darlin', come in and eat. I have a surprise outing for you after dinner."

"Where?" She asks, turning around so fast she slaps me with her hair and it actually stings.

"You'll see, Darlin'. Now, let's go eat."

CHAPTER 28

LUTHER

I didn't tell Rose where we were going for her surprise outing or who would be meeting us there. I want to catch her genuine reaction to the situation and what I have planned. You see, it's easy to tell yourself you are okay with something, and sometimes it's even easier to tell that to someone.

Until you are in it though, you don't truly know. For this to work, I need to truly know she is all in. That when she says she is okay with me being with another man, she actually means it. *That when she says she's okay with Harrison and I testing the waters. That it won't blow up in all of our faces.*

When we pull into the F.O.U.R.S employee lot, Rose looks both shocked and excited. It is almost comical to watch the emotions war with each other on her face. She finally settles on excitement, turning to me and giving me a smile that goes from one side of her face to the other.

"Since I'm coming in with the boss does that mean I get to see behind the curtain?" She asks me with glee.

"We can be back there for a bit, but it's nothing spectacular. Can't stay for too long, though, because I have plans for my lady this evening." Winking at her, I hop out of the car.

Walkin around the hood to her side, I open her door to let her out. She pouts up at me, as she stands. "You know I can get the door myself right?"

Leaning in, I press her body against the door with mine. "Yes, Darlin', I am well aware that you can get your own door. However, just because you can do it doesn't mean you should. You deserve to be treated like the queen you are and when you are with me you will be. Do you understand?"

She lets out a whimper that goes straight to my cock, her voice is husky when she answers me, "Yes, Daddy, I understand."

Unable to resist the temptation that she is, I slide my hand under her dress. Running my middle and forefingers up the inner part of her thigh, I lean into her ear and whisper, "Such a good girl for your Daddy. You did so well waiting for me like I asked you to."

I move my fingers higher, just before I would reach the apex of her thighs. She's slick even here, causing me to groan. "So very wet for me, Minx. You're already dripping down your thighs. Whatever shall we do about that?"

"Daddy," she gasps, "pllleeeaassee"

"Fuck baby, I love to hear you beg." Her fingers tighten where they rest on my hip. Just as I start to move my fingers to her core, a car pulls into the lot and into the spot next to mine.

We both groan at the same time and I let my hand fall

away. I know who will be exiting that car momentarily, and there will be no escaping the chat to follow.

"Well, well if it isn't my favorite brother! What are you doing here?" Xavier calls out as he goes to open Nyla's door.

"Hey Xai, I assume the same as you. Seeing as it isn't either of our weekends to run the show." Looking back down, I see Rose has herself readjusted. Taking a step back from her, I lean down and whisper in her ear, "Soon, I promise."

I lift my head just in time to see Nyla rounding our cars to come speak with us. Xavier's not far behind her, but he's too interested in staring at her ass in the skin tight dress she's wearing, to even notice the vision of a woman next to me.

Stopping in front of us, Nyla gives me a quick hey before bumping me out of the way and pulls Rose in for a hug. Rose is a good sport about it, either catching on to who is hugging her, or just accepting her fate.

Nyla pulls back and holds Rose out at arms length. "Luther's descriptions of you didn't do you justice. You are an absolutely delicious vision," she gushes.

"I'm Nyla, and this is my husband Xavier." I see the spark of recognition flash in Rose's eyes. *Ahh, so it was an accept your fate situation.* Rose's smile grows from timid to excited, as she introduces herself. "It's great to finally meet you! I have heard so much about you both."

She reaches out a hand to Xavier in greeting, but he swipes it away and pulls her in for a quick hug. Whispering something in her ear as they embrace. As they go to separate she lets out an adorable giggle. "Will do." She says with a wink.

Nyla grabs Rose's hand and starts to lead her away. "Um,

excuse me, where do you think you're taking my girlfriend?" I call out.

"With me! You snooze you loose, asshole!" Nyla yells back. Rose, being the sweet little brat she is, looks back to where Xavier and I walk behind them. I can see the slight trepidation in her eyes, but she surprises me and wiggles her eyebrows at me suggestively.

Xavier must catch it too, because we both burst out in laughter at the same time. His hand comes down on my shoulder, "My wife may be Mrs. Steal Your Girl, but it looks like you might have a handful on your hands too."

Walking in the guest entrance of your own club is always a strange feeling, but since Rose doesn't have her new band yet, we didn't want to cause any issues. Even when we do bring guests they aren't allowed in the off limits area.

Staff all wear white bands giving them access to those areas. Everyone else has specific colors based on their availability or designation.

Laura is at the check in desk, the adorable Little Girl who also happens to be Jamie's best friend is always full of energy and is great with members. Dante, our head of security and her Daddy, is next to her. He always works the entrance when she's up here.

She squeals when she sees us. When she rounds the desk, I'm sure she's about to tackle Nyla like she loves to do but instead she charges at Rose. She's ready for it though, dropping Nylas hand just in time. The embrace is met with a 'humph' and a giggle from Rose.

"OMG-EEE," Laura squeals, still squeezing her and

rocking back and forth. "What are you doin' wifs the boss mans?" She asks with the enthusiasm only a Little has.

"I can't breathe, sweets," Rose rasps out. Laura loosens her grip just slightly, but not enough. Dante steps in before Rose has to ask again. "Laura Ann, let go of the poor girl. You're supposed to be checking her in."

Letting her go, she gives her a small, "Sowwy," and heads back behind the counter. "So, obvs I don't need yous threes to scans in, but I dos need you to, Rose."

Rose steps over and scans her thumb. "Awesome," she says, but when she looks down at the computer she gets a confused look on her face. "What's wrong, sweets?" Rose asks.

"Umms, so I knows you usually has a gold band, but it looks like your info mights has gotten messeds up. Lets me..." I cut in before she finishes her sentence, "It's okay Laura. Her information in the system is correct. You should have a new band for her. I got the update that the ones I ordered were delivered yesterday."

Laura's eyes go wide. "Oh, OOHHH! Yes sir, I'll gets em!" She rushes into the small office off to the side. Rose turns to look at me, confusion written all over her face.

Giving her a small nod and a wink, I point back towards Laura who is now back at the counter. Stepping up next to Rose, I take the band boxes from Laura, turning to hand one off to Xavier.

Laura is already removing Rose's gold band from her wrist. As soon as it's off Rose turns to me. "Give me your wrist, Minx." She is obviously confused but does as I ask.

Taking the onyx and white gold band from its box, I

explain, "Only five people, well now six, wear this band here. My siblings, myself," I meet her eyes as I lock the band in place, "and those that belong to us."

Roses eyes go wide clearly understanding the meaning behind both the bracelet and my words. She is mine and everyone here will now know it.

Both Laura and Rose's mouths are wide open in shock, making the rest of us laugh. Dante's low timber fills the space when he jokes, "You two should close your mouths before you catch something in them." They both turn a glare his way while we all laugh again. Before she can turn around again I step up behind her and whisper in her ear, "One can hope."

We say our goodbyes and start to head inside. I signal for the girls to go ahead. Taking the other box from Xavier. Handing it to Dante, I give him instructions then head inside.

The girls are already in our booth when I make it inside, talking like old friends. I watch them for a moment, an indulgent smile on my face. Rose keeps looking down at her wrist and smiling.

Happy with how the night is going so far, I go to meet my brother at the bar. Checking my phone on the way I see that Harrison is about fifteen minutes out.

"That was smooth as hell, big bro," Xai says when I reach him. "Ha, thanks. I told her tonight would be a night for surprises. I just didn't think you two would be one of them," I say to him.

"Don't worry, we aren't here to ruin your mojo. I didn't expect to see you here tonight, either. I thought this was going down next weekend." I just shrug.

Miranda comes over and takes our drink orders and lets

us know she will have one of the servers run it over. With that, we head over to our women.

All of the drinks are delivered a few minutes later and we each take ours. "That's weird, they brought an extra," Nyla points out. I smirk her way, "Not an extra, sis. I have another party meeting us in," I look down at my watch, "roughly four minutes."

Both girls look at me confused, but Xai takes care of his wife for me, "That's our cue to make ourselves scarce, pet. Grab your drink and lets go." Nylas entire demeanor shifts immediately at his demand, "Yes, Master." Before she stands, she turns to Rose, "I'll see you tomorrow at Sunday dinner, right?"

Shit, I forgot to tell her earlier with everything else! Rose looks over at me and I lift my eyebrow while giving her a small nod. Letting her know that it's her decision, as well as giving her permission to answer. "Um, we haven't talked about it yet, but I don't see why I wouldn't." *Good answer, baby.* With another quick hug, Nyla picks up her drink and they head off to do their own thing.

As soon as they are out of ear shot, Rose turns her attention back to me. This time it's her eyebrow raised in question, "Another party, is this part of your plan?"

I nod, but don't get anything else out as my attention is caught by the person walking in the main door. I know the moment he sees me looking at him. His hand goes to his wrist, touching his updated band. For a moment, I was worried he would deny it and request a singles band. The relief I feel, at seeing he didn't, is jarring. The band on his wrist is the same as the one I just gave Rose. The same as all of ours. He accepted the claim by the Breedlove family, but was it only for her? *Or could he really feel and be curious about this 'energy' between us, too?*

Rose notices where my eyes are and turns to see what I'm looking at. Harrison reaches the table right as she starts to turn, and I watch her eyes light up with both surprise and delight. We both stand in greeting. Rose hugs him and immediately starts asking him what he's doing here tonight and asking who he's with.

I don't give him time to answer, instead telling him, "Your drink is already here. Why don't you have a seat and we'll have a talk?"

"How was the concert?" I ask, once we are all settled back in the booth.

"Eh, it was fine. Kat got a bit overwhelmed, but she did great." Looking down, he fidgets with his band.

Rose lets out a gasp and grabs his hand. Her eyes fly up to meet mine and I smile.

"What's this all about, Luther?" He asks me.

Rose chimes in next, "Yes, inquiring minds want to know."

Swirling the drink in my glass, I look directly into Harrison's eyes. "Harrison, tell me how long have you and Rose been play partners?"

He looks taken aback but answers, "Twoish years, why?"

"And you're a switch, yes?" I continue.

Rose's eyes narrow slightly, but then she must catch on to where I'm going with this. "Again, yes, but why?" he asks.

Looking over at Rose, I smirk, "I promised you I would

never take him away from you didn't I?" Her voice is airy when she answers. "You did."

I turn back and look at Harrison, "Do you feel this energy between us? Almost like magnets fighting not to connect? Tell me you don't and I won't say anything else. But if you do..." I let my words trail off. Taking a sip of my drink and giving him a moment to think.

Rose reaches over and squeezes his hand. When their eyes meet, she gives him a look that would melt anyone's heart. I watch as he breathes in deep before turning back to me.

"I feel it too, okay? I'm not sure what it means or what I want from it, but I do feel it, too." He is so flustered, the hand that is holding his drink is trembling. Pointing down at it, I signal him to take a sip. I watch as he takes it all in with one large swallow. Savoring the burn as it goes down. After a moment, he sets his drink down and brings his eyes back to mine.

Bracing myself for the possibility of rejection, I spit out my idea. "I have a proposal for you. That is, if you're open to it." He waves me forward, obviously at a loss for words for the moment. "I would like to propose that at least for tonight, I top both of you." Another gasp leaves Rose's lips, and Harrison looks stunned.

I keep going not wanting to loose my nerve, "I know you mentioned before that you have never been with a man. What I'm trying to say, and doing a horrible job at it, is that if you're up to it, I would like to be your first."

Harrisons face is a mixture of emotions, fear, nervousness, conflict, but the most prevalent emotions I see are pure lust and hunger.

It takes him a moment, but his wheels finally start turning again. I've already started accepting his rejection in my mind when he finally stammers out, "Y-You want to t-top both of us...tonight?"

Followed by Rose immediately asking, "Luther, really? Are you sure? Do you really want that?"

Smirking, I address both of their questions with one answer. Eyes locked on Harrison, I say, "If Harrison thinks he's up for it, yeah."

I can see he is still on the fence, "But this is y'all's first night together right?"

My smirk deepens, my voice is almost so low even I barely recognize it. "Ah, and now you've stumbled upon why I feel it is so important to do this together."

I lean forward into his space, never taking my eyes off his. Letting my own lust burn through, so he can see just how bad I want this. Want him.

"I want you to show me. Show me all of the buttons that set our girl aflame. Show me the places that make her toes curl and the areas that when you touch them cause her whole body to tremble. I want you to show me every spot no matter how big or small."

Letting my smirk turn into the full blown predator smile I have been fighting. I growl, "By the time we leave this club tonight, I want a puddle on the floor and neither of you to be walking properly."

Harrisons eyes are huge, but I can see he understands what I'm telling him. Even as he asks, "Neither of us?"

"Yes, Harrison, if you agree to this, you are agreeing to not just being with her tonight, but with me as well. We can discuss your limits if you would like, and I will always respect them. I should also let you know that I've already seen and reviewed your paperwork. Thoroughly." I say.

Emboldened by the lust I see in him, I move forward, erasing the rest of the distance between us.

With a groan I whisper in his ear for him alone, "If you agree to this....she won't be the only one that will be flowing tonight."

CHAPTER 29

HARRISON

*I*s this really happening? Am I going to agree to be with a man? My mind is running a mile a minute. I feel Rose reach over and squeeze my hand. "You know you don't have to do this, if you don't want to or if you're not ready, right?" Smiling at her, I tell her, "I know, but I want to."

From his spot in the booth, Luther says, "Even if we get in there and you decide, in that moment, that you don't want to play with me, that you only want to touch her. That's okay, too. Remember, any consent given can be taken away at any time."

I don't want to live in fear of the unknown. There's something between me and Luther that I just can't explain and I want to experience it so badly. Looking him in the eyes, I nod and then turn to Rose. "I can't promise anything more than tonight. I'll try, okay, but I don't know if I'll like it."

Turning back to Luther, I ask, "How exactly is this going to work?" With that sexually devious smile of his, he says, "I'll need you to follow. It'll be just like it would be if you were with a female dominant. I'll take care of you both."

I'm not sure what it is about Luther, but it looks like I'm going to find out. Both Luther and Rose finish their drinks quickly after that and we stand. "Where are we going?" I ask Luther.

"I felt that you would be the most comfortable going back to the room we were in last time. That way it's just us and you can experience this in your own way, without expectations or an audience." Now I know what Rose means when you get butterflies in your stomach just from somebody thinking about your feelings first.

Following behind Luther, my mind is occupied with what might happen in the voyeur room and in the future. Since most of my encounters have been with submissives, it's rare that I get to indulge in my own submissive side.

With Rose, it's been easy to share my full self and still lead during our scenes. Doesn't hurt that I've been secretly in love with her for years. She's just never seen me that way.

There have been times that made me question if she has feelings for me, but I've never said anything for fear of losing my best friend. Now that she's with Luther, I prepared myself for losing my submissive but keeping my friend. What's at the front of my thoughts at this moment, is if this night could ruin everything for us?

Walking down the same hallway we were in last time, my mindset is different. I'm not trying to plan the scene. I'm not trying to choose the hows and wheres. I'm able to just be. Everywhere I look, there are writhing bodies, but none of them interest me as much as the two people in front of me. I

When we reach the private room, Luther unlocks the door and leads us in.

"Both of you have a seat," looking at each other, we smile and follow instructions. I have to remember that tonight I follow, I don't lead. Luther turns to address us both, "Before we start, is there anything you don't want me to do?"

Looking him in the eyes, I clear my throat before saying, "At least for tonight, no pain. I don't want to associate this with pain. Is that okay?" He looks at me and smiles softly. "Absolutely! There will never be a time that I'll tell you something you don't want to happen is wrong. Now, there may be times where I don't want to do or try something you want, but that's normal, right? You know that as a dominant." I nod my head at him. "All right, both of you," he says to us. "Color checks"

"Green," says Rose.

"I'm green, as well." I say.

"Okay, then. Do you have a specific safeword that you'd like to use or are you both okay with, for tonight, using colors?" Nodding I say, "I'm good with that," then move my attention to Rose. I check with her, "Are you okay with that?" She smiles at me, "I am perfectly okay with the stop light system." As soon as those words come out of her mouth, Luther's entire demeanor changes.

"Both of you stand." He demands. We rise to our feet waiting for his next command. "Strip. While I prepare a few things." We both nod and I feel a shiver of trepidation crawl up my spine. I close my eyes for a few seconds to clear my mind and settle myself to be in the moment. When I open them again, Rose is staring at me. "I'll help you, okay. I'm right here with you." She whispers. Taking that as a good sign, I begin to undress. By the time Luther comes back to our side of the room, I'm completely nude and Rose is just standing in her black lace thong.

He's staring directly into my eyes, when she moves to remove the thong. "Stop!" He says. "Harrison, go over to Rose." So I do. "Now, on your knees." Lowering myself in front of her, heat flares up my spine. I can smell just how aroused she actually is.

My cock is hard as steel and all I can think is, *I hope he lets me get a taste.* "Pull down her underwear." He commands me. Reaching over, I grabbed both sides and slowly lower her thong to the floor. "Good," He says, "Now, show me how you would make her come."

Taking Rose's hand, I turn her so her back is to the couch. Thankfully, the couch is huge, so she's able to just turn. Pressing my hand against the soft flesh of her belly, I help her sit, legs spread.

Out of the corner of my eye, I see Luther set down a small basket on the side table. The sight of the packets that are sitting on top makes me freeze. I shake my head at him and he responds with a confused look. "Um, we don't use condoms. There's something in them that causes issues for me. I'm clean though, I've stayed up to date with the required testing for the club, and Rose is the only one I've been with in over a year." Understanding crosses his face. "Okay, I'm okay with that. Are you both okay with me being bare? I was just tested a few weeks ago and you two are the only ones I've done anything with in that time."

"I'm fine with that," Rose says before smiling down at

me. I'm caught off guard when Luther clears his throat, his eyes on mine, asking "And you?" I pause and process the question. It isn't until then that I understand that there is a very good chance he will fuck me tonight. The thought makes my hole tense but my cock pulse. "You can go without, uhmmm...what should I call you?" I'm stuck on what to call him. "Sir, tonight you can call me Sir."

Nodding, I turn my attention back to Rose. "Now, since we had to pause for some unexpected housekeeping. I'll tell you again. Show me how you bring our girl to ecstasy."

At his command, I lift my hand to Rose's chest gently pushing her to lie back. I hear her breath catch, and I know it's because of the position she is in. Exposed to us both, pussy dripping with need. Her nipples pebble in the cool air of the room and I slide my hands down her legs stopping behind her knees. Lifting her legs, I set them on my shoulders.

Turning my head, I bite the inside of her thigh. Rose lets out a deep moan. Turning my head I do it again, but harder, on the other side. "Harrison," she moans out. Pausing, I ask, "Yes, Sweetheart." She groans deep in her throat. "Please, don't tease me. Daddy's been doing it all night." I let out a chuckle, "Careful what you say, Sweetheart. He's the one in charge tonight."

Those words do something to me. The thought of him owning both of us, along with her whimpers, makes me groan. She must feel it too, because she lets out a mewling whimper at the same time. Deciding not to focus on that too much for now, I lean forward and slowly start to lick her pussy. She's always tasted so sweet to me, but still has that essence that is just purely feminine. I circle her entrance with my tongue and her back arches off the bed.

"Fuck," she lets out, "That feels so damn good!" I move further up her slit and circle her clit with the tip of my tongue. "Oh, Harrison," she whimpers out again.

From behind me, I hear the rustle of clothes being removed. "Good boy! I want you to bring her all the way to the edge, but don't take her off the cliff, yet." I do as he said. Sliding two fingers deep within her, I curl them up, while sucking on her clit. I can feel her tightening around my fingers as I rub that soft spot inside of her. "Oh, God! Oh, God! Harrison, please!"

"Stop." I hear from behind me and I stop immediately. "You seem to forget who's in charge this evening, Minx."

"No, Daddy," she says. "I didn't forget."

"Then why are you begging Harrison and not me?" I can hear the warning in his voice, and it causes a delicious reaction throughout my body. She pauses, knowing she's messed up, but trying to figure out how to get out of it.

"Well, Daddy. If I'm being honest, he's the only one who's ever eaten my pussy in this room." I hear Luther growl from close behind me. "You are right about that, Minx. I guess we're going to have to change that now, aren't we?" *Fuck, that's hot!!*

"Bend over, Minx. Hands and knees." She doesn't waste any time adjusting her position like he asks. "Harrison, on your feet." Rising from where I'm seated on the floor, I stand behind Rose. "Now, I am going to eat this pussy and you are going to fuck it."

Rose lets out a moan that makes my cock twitch and

throb. "Fuck, Sweetheart. If you keep making sounds like that, I won't last." Tilting my head backward to try and gain composure, I'm caught off guard when I feel Luther lower down to the floor between my legs. Just knowing I'll see his face when I look down, is enough to make my cock begin to twitch more. I can feel the pre-cum weeping from me.

When I feel his warm tongue against my shaft, I know I'm done for, before I even got started. He licks me from base to tip, before circling my head with his tongue. Shivers shoot through my entire body at the feeling, and a whine leaves me. "You want more?" he asks, his lips gently rubbing against my tip as he speaks. "Or do you want me to stop?"

I feel like my heart stops. It's now or never, either I'm in or I'm out. "Please, don't stop," I tell him, breathlessly. "Open your eyes and look at me," he says. The order in his tone is clear. Taking a deep inhale, I look down at the beautiful man sitting beneath me. "That's a good boy," my cock jumps at his praise, making even more pre-cum leak from me. It feels like I'm watching a movie in slow motion as I watch him lean forward and lick off the resulting bead from the tip. "Are you already on the edge, baby?"

I'm panting, ready to blow after barely being touched. "Y-yes, Sir, I'm trying, really I am." He reaches up and cups my balls in his hand. Gasping from the zap of electricity that runs through me at his touch, I moan out, "Fuck, I am so close."

"Inside me," Rose says in a husky voice, "please." It only takes Luther a second to come up with a plan. "You heard her, baby. Better get to work," Confused, I ask, "What do you mean?"

Luther slides his other hand up the back of my thigh, as he releases my balls and grabs my hips. Gently he pulls them forward, as he says, "I mean, get inside of her."

Taking a step forward, I grip my base. I watch Luther's head disappear under her right before I sink inside. I shudder and pant, as I slide inside of her. When I finally bottom out, I take a moment to just feel her surrounding me. The feeling of her tight wet pussy surrounding my cock makes my knees weak.

My hands run up her back and I start moving slowly, using long deep strokes, giving her time to adjust to the intrusion. Luthers hands move from my hips to hers, and she shudders under my hands.

Her breaths are ragged as I move, and I know the exact moment his mouth makes contact with her pussy. She lets out a deep moan, and clamps down on me so hard, she almost throws me over the edge. "Ooohh, fffuucckk! Daddy! Harrison! That feels so fucking good!" She's already quickly on her way to her first orgasm.

I'm not sure what he's doing to her, but her pussy is convulsing so much I'm already about to explode. "Sir, I'm going to cum, please may I cum?" I pant out, only making her clamp down harder. My back bows and my balls start to draw up at the feeling. I'm fighting a losing battle trying not to cum.

"Cum, both of you, cum now," He says. Quickly going back to devouring her pussy. I can feel his tongue as I pick up speed. My balls slapping his chin every time I bottom out. My balls draw up the rest of the way, and I thrust in deep, holding myself there.

Just as I do, Rose clamps hard screaming out her orgasm and Luther reaches up and gently tugs my balls. The mixture of sensations as I fill her makes me see stars and my vision waivers.

Luther's grip loosens as I come back to reality. Rose's pussy is still fluttering around me as I begin to pull out of her. Luther drags his tongue along the underside as I go and as my cock leaves her heat, Luther surrounds it.

Sucking me in, he swirls his tongue, tasting Roses and my mixed arousal. The feeling of his mouth on me so soon after release is intense and too much for me to handle. "Sir, please," I beg him. Popping off of me, he hums and licks his lips. "Go sit by her head," he orders. Once I'm no longer standing over him he shifts, rising to his knees, he smacks Rose's ass before telling her, "On your back, Minx."

Taking a seat, I watch Rose collapse and roll over. Luther pushes open her legs and centers himself between them. Lowering his face, he pauses just before he reaches her core. "Daddy's going to clean up your boy's mess, and I won't be stopping until you're clean. You can cum however many times you'd like." His eyes move to me, "You can touch her, but you can't touch yourself and she can't touch you."

With that he doesn't waste anymore time, diving into her like a man starved. Running his tongue from her taint to her clit, with a moan. She's shivering as he devours every bit of her pussy, like a starving man at a buffet

When he's satisfied, he spears her with his tongue, making her scream. Watching him feast is amazing. He's sucking our juices out of her while fucking her with his tongue. Seemingly not wanting to miss a single drop of our combined release.

Her body tenses and she screams, "FUCK DADDY! YES DADDY, RIGHT THERE!" Her back arches as she comes apart on his tongue.

My cock is already hard again between my legs, the scene before me is dirty and sexy. I need more. Leaning over her body, my fingertips caress Rose's cheek. Bending, my lips graze hers, in a gentle kiss. Her eyes grow wide with excited anticipation as my hand moves slowly lower, over her breasts and belly, descending to her clit. I begin rubbing the small powerful bud.

Moving to where I can still watch him, I gently blow on her nipple making her shiver, and her nipples to harden further. Sucking it into my mouth, she begins to shutter, crying out, "Oh fuck, Harrison," Seeing how deep she already is in her pleasure, Luther pushes her legs up further. I watch as he sinks two fingers into her pussy, and lowers his face further. I can no longer see his face and I have a feeling I know what he is doing with that sinful mouth of his.

Adjusting to her other breast, I work her clit in tight circles, watching the emotions play across her face. Her eyes are closed, her head thrown back, grinding her pussy down on to him. Reaching over with my free hand I wrap it around her throat, squeezing at the same time that I bite down. She detonates, screaming incoherent words as her release takes over.

I look down just in time to watch as she sprays her release. I release her throat, and she gasps a breath. Luther is relentless though, never stopping the movements of his fingers as he adjusts himself to lean over her, pushing her legs even further back. "Again baby, give me another one, Minx." Her body is shaking as she cums again, this time soaking Luther's stomach with her release.

I continue rubbing her clit gently, letting her fully ride the tsunami of an orgasm that she just experienced. When she stops shaking, I remove my hand from her clit and kiss her lips.

Luther's growl sends a shiver down my spine, as he rises from the floor. "You were both so good for me, that was beautiful." He takes another step towards me, "I think you deserve a reward, don't you?"

Nodding, I breathe out, "Please, Sir." He takes another step, close enough now that I can feel the heat of his body and smell the scent of her release from where it's glistening on the skin of his well cut abs. Taking my chin in his hand, he grips it tightly bending my neck so I'm looking up at him. Moving his hand from my chin, he grabs my throat, using his grip to pull me closer and takes my mouth with his.

His mouth is like nothing I've ever felt being with a woman. His lips are still soft, but they are wide and commanding. He flicks his tongue against my top lip, and I open for him. As soon as I do, he sinks his tongue into my mouth.

The kiss is almost feral, biting, licking, he takes my mouth like he took her pussy. The feeling pushing me into a vortex of desire I've never experienced.

Using his body, he lowers me to my back on the couch. He moves his mouth down to my chin giving it a slight nip before continuing his descent. He moves his hand down my body and between my spread legs. His hand slides between my cheeks and starts to rub his finger around my virgin hole. "Are you going to be a good boy and let me take this ass, baby?"

I tense for just a moment, but then nod. "Words, Harrison. I need your words for this or I'll stop right here."

My back arches as the command in his voice mixes with the pleasurable feeling of him rubbing my hole. "Yes Sir, please take me." He places another kiss on my lips. "Good boy, you're so obedient for me." Looking over his shoulder he addresses Rose. "Are you okay with this, Minx?"

"Hell yeah, this is fucking sexy as hell." She splutters. "I'm glad to hear it. Please bring me the bottle of lube that's in the basket." Standing, she grabs the bottle like he asked and walks over to us. Opening it she dribbles it between my legs. I feel his slippery fingers slide across my hole and tense up again.

He pulls back from the kiss and kisses down my neck. "Relax," the moment he feels me relax, he slides his finger in. "Ffffuuuuccccckkkk..." I groan, my body shutters at the foreign feeling. "There you go, baby," I groan at the sensations. "How does it feel?" I shiver, "It...it feels so full," my voice is more of a whimper. He draws his finger back, pumping it in again slowly. "Are you ready for another?" He asks me. "Umm I think so," I pant out, trying not to panic.

"Minx, help him out," nodding his head towards my cock. She sucks my cock to the back of her throat at the same time that Luther adds a second finger. The burning sensation of being stretched is almost too much, but mixed with the feel of Rose's mouth around my cock, it's bearable. He slowly works his fingers deeper into me, spreading them as he does. Rose slowly sucks me through it all. When he rubs against something inside of me, a wave of pleasure hits me so strong that I can feel it in my fucking toes. "HOLY SHITTTT, SIR! FUCKKKKK, THAT FEELS SO DAMN GOOD, SHIT!!" I cry out, feeling overwhelmed by the pleasure.

He lets out a small chuckle, "That's it, baby, feel me stretching you out to take my cock." I groan, it's so much but it's also not enough. "Sir, please," I beg. "Are you ready for me baby?" I grunt as he hits that magic spot once again. "YES, PLEASE! FUCK, SIR." I know I must not be making sense, but I feel Luther adjust to pick up the bottle again. I hear the cap open before I feel the cool liquid running between my cheeks, his fingers fucking it into me deeper.

Luther moves so he can get in position and Rose pulls off of me and leans back. Taking me in her hand she starts to slowly stroke. Leaning down to my ear she whispers, "I am so excited to watch you take him. Breathe, and push back on him when he pushes in." Nodding, I feel him slide his fingers from me. I feel oddly empty at the loss of his fingers, but then I feel him move as he lines himself up with my asshole. He pauses and our eyes meet. "One last time. Are you sure?" I can see the hunger burning behind his eyes, but also the sincerity. If I tell him to stop now he would. I don't want him to stop though.

I have to take several calming breaths, before I answer, "Please don't stop, Sir. Please fuck me." As soon as the words leave my lips he pushes his hips forward, and I feel the head of his cock slide in. He goes slow so he doesn't hurt me. Until my tight ring of muscle slowly opens and allows him inside. I shudder and pant, until I finally feel his pubic bone come to rest against my ass.

I feel so fucking full, and it's burns. I feel my body begin to accept his intrusion and he must feel it too because he starts pumping his hips in me in short deep strokes. He's rubbing my prostate with every slow drag in and out, making my whole body light up with fireworks. "You feel fucking incredible, baby. You're taking my cock so well."

His praise sends tingles down my spine. My head falls back, in a gasp of pleasure. My hands grip at his massive shoulder and I whimper softly when he starts moving with harder, long strokes, deep into my unbelievably tightly stretched ass. It feels so good, my spine is so tight, it feels like it's liable to snap. "Fuck baby, I want to pound your ass so fucking hard. I want to ride you like a dirty slut until you shatter for me."

I whimper at his words and my ass clenches around him, "I think someone likes the idea of being my dirty little cock slut. Look at you, your cock is absolutely weeping at the idea." He starts driving into me harder and I can't stop the loud moans coming from me. "Fuck Sir, Please...you feel good," He leans back a bit making my hand fall from his shoulder, but now driving his cock directly into that spot that has my body alight with pleasure.

"Rose, why don't you help this dirty boy out and clean him up with your mouth?" Rose leans forward, and takes me in deep. "FuckFuckFuckFuckFuck, Sir! I'M GONNA CUM!" He grunts and begins to pound into me. "Cum for me, baby!" And I do! I cum so hard that the last thing I hear before I pass out is him groaning his release.

I'm not sure how long I'm out for, but I wake up to the feel of something soft and wet running between my cheeks. "Shhh, I'm just cleaning you up." Luther coos to me. When he finishes he brings my clothes over to where I'm sitting. "I want you both to stay with me tonight." I look at Rose and she nods. Dressing, I follow them out to Luther's car, I'm exhausted and ready for sleep.

CHAPTER 30

✧

ROSE

My phone's incessant vibrating on the nightstand tears me from sleep. The light coming in through the windows tells me it is way too early to be awake, especially with how late we were out last night. Checking the screen, I see it's my mother calling me. *No, no, no, it is way too early for this.* Hitting decline, I pull myself out of bed trying everything in my power to not wake up either of the guys. Reaching down, I grab a shirt off the floor and grab my phone.

Checking the time on my phone, I see it's just before seven in the morning. The fact she even entertained calling me this early on a Sunday, proves she is insane. Stopping by the bathroom before leaving the room, I quickly pee, wash my hands and face, and brush my teeth. There's no way I'm going back to sleep now so I might as well wake up fully. I leave the room as quietly as I can and head to make the nectar of the gods.

I have barely even started the coffee pot when my phone

rings again. *Dammit, this woman is determined to piss me off before I'm even functional today! Fuck it, she gets no filter uncaffeinated Rose then...*

"Morning, Mother," I know I sound bitchy but I just can't bring myself to care.

"Well, good morning daughter. Nice of you to answer your phone. What if this was me calling you to tell you I was hurt and you ignored my calls? How would you feel?"

Oh, we are doing the guilt trip thing this morning.

"Well, are you calling to tell me you're hurt?"

She huffs, "No, Rose Marie, I am not."

Yeah, I didn't think so, "What can I help you with this morning, Mother?"

"First things first, you can drop the attitude,"

Ugh.

"Second, you can explain to me why the wonderful birthday gifts I gave you are still unused! I put a lot of thought into that gift and you are just blowing it off! You will never find a good decent man, like you want, unless you do something about your weight! You can not stay an FG for the rest of your life, Rose!"

My stomach churns at her words. Fat girl or FG as she likes to call it has been my mother's go to 'pet name' for my weight since I was little. The woman put me on every fad diet she found over the years, never just being okay with who I am but wanting me to be skinnier. When I moved out the pokes at my weight continued, but she didn't start using finding a husband against me till last year. *Well, if he doesn't want me or loves me for who I am, then I don't want him.* I need coffee.

Putting my phone on speaker, I set it down and turn to the now full pot.

"Mother, I told you when you gave them to me that I wasn't interested. I am the size that I am. Hell, I've been a size 18 since my junior year of high school. I don't think that is going to change. I've accepted my body. Why can't you?"

She makes some form of weird groan sound. "You want me to accept my daughter being obese? I think not. You're a pretty girl, Rose, and I just want what's best for you. If we can get you to a healthy size, I'm positive we can find you a husband."

"Mother, I do not need to lose weight to find a man," *or woman*, "Honestly, if they don't want and love me for who I am at any size that I am...well, to be blunt I don't want them at all. I'm active, I eat normally, and I take care of myself. Leave it alone." I growl out the last bit of that statement. I hate that she can't just love me as I am.

"Ughh, Rose, I am so disappointed. With fantasies like that, I'll never be a grandmother!"

"Was there anything else you wanted to attack me with this morning, Mother?"

Under her breath I hear her growl out, "I should have spanked you more as a child." Will this woman never learn that I can hear her? It's calls like this that make me glad I decided to move 16 hours away from home.

"Mother?"

"Rose Marie, I don't know why you have to always be so dramatic making out like I'm attacking you. I have nothing else I would like to discuss with you this morning."

"Always lovely speaking with you, Mother. Goodbye."

BREATHE

I don't even wait for her to say her goodbyes before I hang up. Slumping against the counter, I sip my coffee. I think this might end up being a quad espresso at noon kind of day.

Hands wrap around me from behind startling me momentarily. "I like waking up to you in my kitchen." Luther says, before kissing me on the shoulder. "What I don't like is what ever the fuck I just heard spewing out of that bitch's mouth."

Turning in his arms, I shrug and bury my face in his chest. "That's normal, I've never been enough for her. At least through the phone she can't hit me for saying I don't want something."

Luther uses his finger to bring my face up to look into his eyes. "Darlin', you are more than enough. You are everything." He bends down and takes my mouth with his. My arms slide up his chest and around his neck as I let out a groan of contentment. Luther slides his hands down my back, to my ass.

Using his grip he lifts me and sets me on the counter. I'm only wearing one of his t-shirts that he gave me to sleep in last night, so my pussy is exposed and already dripping for him. Reaching under the hem, I groan when Luther rubs his fingers along my wet slit, before pushing them deep inside.

A throat clears from behind us putting a stop to our little dance of tongues, "Well, good morning, you two," Harrison says from where he stands near the island.

"Morning, Baby," Both me and Luther look at him and say at the same time. My tone is sassy and breathy, while Luther's sounds hungry.

"Oh, I'm Baby now, am I? I thought that was just a last

night thing?" His words sound like he's playing, but his eyes give him away. He's worried that last night was a fluke. Before I can say anything Luther pulls his fingers from me and walks over to Harrison. Grabbing him by the back of the neck, Luther slams his mouth to Harrison's.

Harrison lets out a whimper at the action, but doesn't stop him. No, instead his hands wrap around Luther's waist and his hands grip Luther's ass. Luther lets out a groan that makes shivers run down my spine and I'm not even the one he's claiming at the moment.

Pulling away, Luther takes Harrison's hand and brings him over to me. With my legs still spread he easily maneuvers him to stand between them before moving to stand behind him. "Morning, Baby," I say, leaning in and kissing him for myself.

His mouth tastes like mint and Harrison, and home. He runs his hands up my legs jerking me towards the edge of the counter. I can feel his hard length between us and I want it inside me more than I think I've ever wanted coffee. *What the fuck are these two doing to me?*

"You feel this?" Luther asks, grinding his hips into Harrison, "This is what you do to me." Harrison lets out a moan at the feeling. I know his ass has to be sore today, but I can tell he wants it.

"You feel this?" Luther asks, sliding Harrison's hand to my dripping slit and we both moan, "This is what you do to her." Harrison slides his fingers inside of me and starts working my pussy with vigor. "Don't doubt the way we feel about you, Baby. You are OURS."

Luther's voice is a growl as he says those words. My pussy

suddenly clenches and I'm cumming all over Harrison's hand. When he pulls his hand free, Luther lifts it, placing Harrison's fingers in his own mouth and sucking my juices off of them.

I don't get to enjoy it though, as my phone rings beside me again. Looking down at the disrespectful device as I see 'Birth Giver' flashing across the screen.

The growl Luther lets out this time is angry, as he tells me, "Put it on speaker."

Doing as I'm told, I answer the phone, "What, Mother?"

"You are so rude, Rose Marie." She snaps and I roll my eyes.

"Do you need something or are you just calling to disrespect me some more?" I ask, angry that she's ruining what should be a beautiful morning with two of the hottest men on this planet.

"I have decided you are coming home, whether you like it or not. It's obvious you are incapable or taking care of yourself and are having a mental break. Pack your things, it's time for you to get your life and priorities together and come home."

My jaw drops, I can't believe this woman's audacity! Before I can say a word, Luther has snatched up my phone. "Good morning, Ms. Morrow. This is Luther Breedlove."

I hear my mother let out a small gasp. She quickly gains her composure and snaps, "I don't care who you are sir. Just let me speak to my daughter."

Luther shakes his head as he says, "I think you have done enough talking for one day, ma'am. You are being extremely disrespectful to my woman and I will not stand for that."

"She is my daughter and I will speak to her anyway I

damn well please. I don't care who you are or what you think you are to her, but you have no right to tell me how I can speak to my daughter!" She's shrieking and the sound makes me flinch.

"Listen to me and listen well, I have every right to tell you how you can and can't speak to her. As a man, I protect what's mine and since she is mine. I have every right to protect her. Until you can speak to Rose in a respectful manner, I think it's best if you two don't speak at all." He emphasizes the word 'mine' to get his point across.

He's claiming me, protecting me, doing something for me that no one has ever done before. I feel the tears running down my face, and Harrison wraps his arm around me, pulling my face to his chest.

Luther hangs up the phone as she starts shrieking again, about how we are going to regret this or something along those lines. I don't hear it, though, as I sit there bawling into Harrison's chest.

I feel Luther's hands run through my hair, as I cry. It isn't until I calm down and pull back from Harrison that I see just how concerned Luther is for me. Reaching out, I take his cheek in my hand. "Thank you, Daddy. No one has ever stuck up for me with her like that before."

He leans down, pressing a gentle kiss to my lips. "I meant every word, Darlin'. We are here to protect you, that's our job, as your men. To protect, to cherish, to love. I can tell you haven't had much of that in your life. But moving forward, you will. Let us help take the burdens weighing you down. Let us lift you up when you feel like you're drowning. Let us show you that you are enough, and that woman's full of shit."

He pauses, staring me right in the eye. "Let us help you breathe."

Helping me down, Luther starts to lead me to the bedroom. "Come on, Darlin'. Let's get you into a hot bath, before we have to get ready to go to Nonna's."

I freeze and turn a questioning look at Harrison. He's behind us, two coffee cups in hand, "What is it, BooBear?" he asks looking confused.

"Well, we are supposed to go to Nonna's today," I say and he nods. "What about you?" I ask, my voice quiet but panicked.

Harrison still looks confused by my question. Luther squeezes my hand in his. "He's coming with us, Darlin'. I'm not afraid to show off what's mine, and neither is my family."

Smacking my ass, he continues, "Tub. Now." making Harrison Chuckle. Luther looks back at him and says, "I swear! Woman just needs to breathe!"

EPILOGUE

HARRISON

The last two weeks have been fantastic. Rose and I are at the girls' apartment tonight since Luthers in Houston dealing with their warehouse issue and Kat wanted some bestie time.

We are getting our footing doing this whole throuple thing. Don't get me wrong, us transitioning from being friends to more, has had its difficulties, but as Kat so lovingly pointed out when we told her. Rose and I have basically been together for years.

Luther's family has been great. Nonna is seriously the coolest lady I have ever met. She accepted me instantly and if she keeps feeding me her amazing food, I'm liable to explode. Let's just say, Sundays at her house are...filling.

We are all curled up on the couch watching the new tv adaptation of one of the girls' favorite vampire books series when there's a knock on the door.

Standing, I walk over to the door and check the peephole.

There are two constables standing at the door. Turning to the girls I say, "The police are here."

They both turn to me and look just as confused as I feel. Seeing that I'm not joking, they come around the couch to stand by me. Opening the door, I greet the two officers.

"Afternoon officers, how can I assist you today?" I ask.

The older of the two is the one to answer, "Afternoon, I'm Officer Sharp and this is Officer Taylor, we are looking for Rose Marie Morrow?"

Rose takes a small step forward, still looking confused. "Um, I'm Rose, have I done something wrong?" She looks terrified and I hate it, but I'm not sure what I can do.

"Ma'am, a Mental Health Warrant has been issued for your detainment and transport to Springfield Psychiatric Hospital. We are going to need you to come with us, immediately." He says, reaching his hand out to her in a placating gesture.

"Excuse me? What the hell do you mean? I haven't done anything wrong!" She says panic clearly in her voice.

I move to step in front of her and the older cop sets his hand on his taser.

"Ma'am, it isn't my job to know the whys. All I can tell you is that we are to take you to the airport immediately. Your flight leaves in two hours." He reaches for her again. Grabbing her arm and pulling her to the hallway.

I move to go after them, but the younger officer steps in front of me. "Don't," he whispers to me. "He will just be an asshole to her if you do and legally we have to take her."

Looking down the hall, he sees the other officer staring

back at him. "Take her down to the car, I'm going to get her some shoes and a jacket. I'll meet you down there in a minute. Ma'am, trust me it's best to not fight it and go with him."

She must see the same thing on his face that I do because she stops struggling. She looks defeated and I just want to run to her. Calling out to her, I say, "We will figure this out. I promise. We won't lose our world." I hope she knows what I'm trying to tell her.

She nods and turns to go with the old asshole. Officer Taylor steps into the apartment, and closes the door. "Listen, this whole thing sounded weird to me, too, okay. I don't have a lot of time, so can one of you pack while I explain to the other?" Kat nods at him, "I can."

He smiles down at her, "Good, I really do need to get her some shoes and a jacket. Also any other comfortable clothes you think she might want and medications. If she doesn't already have it on her, I would also say pack her phone and charger, but turn it off and put it at the bottom of the bag."

Kat nods at his instructions and hurries off to get him what he's asked for. "Now, please explain why I just watched my girlfriend get pulled down the hallway for some type of warrant I've never heard of."

Taking a deep breath, Officer Taylor explains that the warrant came from the Missouri constables office claiming that Rose is suffering from suicidal ideations, confusion, depression, withdrawing from her family, and is threatening violence to others.

Pulling out a copy of the warrant he places it in my hand, "You didn't get this from me, okay? But when I saw that she was to be taken to the airport and taken to a facility outside of

Texas, especially with that list of symptoms, it threw up major red flags for me."

My mind is spinning. *What the hell do I do?* "We are on flight 144 at six." Just then Kat walks over and hands him Rose's bag. "Thank you, Angel." He says smiling down at her.

"I have to go, but you should contact a lawyer, but more importantly, DO NOT contact her family." He says, turning towards the door.

"Why shouldn't we contact her family?" Kat asks as his hand grabs the door handle.

He looks back at her with a sad expression, "Because Angel, her family is the one who had that warrant issued." With that he leaves.

Kat whirls to me, "THAT BITCH! What are we going to do?"

I'm already halfway across the room before she finishes her sentence.

Picking up my phone, I dial Luther. He answers on the second ring. "Hey, Baby. What's up?"

My voice comes out in a sob as I answer him.

"Luther, I need your help. They took our Rose."

ACKNOWLEDGMENTS

Wow, thank you so much for making it here. To my readers, thank you for taking a chance on a brand new author with a dream.

I want to give the biggest THANK YOU to my husband and our daughters. You believed in me even when I didn't. You encouraged me to ignore the discouragement and just follow my dream. Supporting me through it all.

To my team behind the scenes, I seriously have no idea what I would have done without y'all.

Samm and Tori - Thank you for listening to me and encouraging me to even dive in.

My Alphas - Thank you for sticking with me and being brutally honest.

Catie - Thank you for staying on video chat with me for hours everyday, encouraging me and keeping me from getting distracted.

Lori - Thank you for not letting me flounder or give up and staying up with me at all hours of the night.

Lastly, I want to thank Ames Mills, Kate Oliver, and Amo Jones for letting me use titles that inspire me in my own story.

ABOUT THE AUTHOR

V.W. Smith was created to craft immersive and inclusive romances that delve into the diverse dynamics of relationships within the BDSM community. Her debut novel, Breathe, is the captivating first installment in the Club F.O.U.R.S. series.

Skillfully explore the theme of Freedom of Ultimate Release and Submission through the lives of the club's patrons and their stories.

Based in Texas, V.W. resides with her husband and spirited daughters. She also has an elusive cat and an exuberant, oversized dog. When not immersed in her loving family or penning tantalizing fantasies, she can be found cultivating her extensive garden or lost in the pages of a compelling book.

Made in the USA
Las Vegas, NV
14 March 2025

88d7f9a7-bce5-4012-990d-397f0e8eda37R01